Jackdaw

ALSO BY TADE THOMPSON

Rosewater
The Rosewater Insurrection
The Rosewater Redemption
Far from the Light of Heaven
Making Wolf
The Murders of Molly Southbourne
The Survival of Molly Southbourne
The Legacy of Molly Southbourne

Jackdaw

Being the memoir
of a most
interesting assignment

Tade Thompson

CHEERIO

CHEERIO

First published in Great Britain in 2022 by
CHEERIO Publishing
www.cheeriopublishing.com
info@cheeriopublishing.com

Copyright © Tade Thompson, 2022

10 9 8 7 6 5 4 3 2 1

Cover design by Jamie Keenan
Printed and bound in Great Britain by Clays Ltd, Elcograf S.p.A.

The moral right of the author has been asserted.
All rights reserved. Without limiting the rights under copyright reserved above, no part of this publication may be reproduced, stored or introduced into a retrieval system, or transmitted, in any form or by any means (electronic, mechanical, photocopying, recording or otherwise), without the prior written permission of both the copyright owner and the publisher of this book.

A CIP catalogue record for this book is available from the British Library.
ISBN: 978 1 7394405 2 7
eISBN: 978 1 8008117 1 3
Audio ISBN: 978 1 8008125 5 0

1

My first connection to Francis Bacon was years earlier.

I returned from work in the evening and headed for the attic, which is where my study was at the time. My friend Camille, ever supportive, called from New York, barely able to contain herself.

'What?' I asked.

'You've made it,' said Camille.

'Made what?'

'You're in the *New York Times*. You've hit the big time.'

'What are you talking about?'

'The *New York Times* reviewed *The Murders of Molly Southbourne*. I swear, I got goose bumps when they compared the feelings induced to those of Francis Bacon's Screaming Popes.'

'You're lying.'

'I'm sending it to you right now. Congratulations!'

Camille wasn't lying.

I considered framing the paper, which was an insert, one should add. It not only compared my book to Francis Bacon, but also to Lucian Freud.

I didn't frame the review, but at times, when the days were longer than twenty-four hours and my patience bottomed out by midday, I would think of it and smile.

Even if I had wanted to frame it, where would I have put it? My study was deliberately spartan. The attic was maybe twelve by fifteen feet, though it was difficult to say because of the irregular shape. I came up by step ladder and the hatch door had a square hole in it. Three flatpack-built bookshelves groaned under the double-stacked weight of my books, next to which I had a desk, which was really an Ikea dining table for a bachelor. I sat on a wooden dining chair, not an ergonomic swivel marvel. I had a reliable desktop. I had a drawing board mounted on two plastic boxes, my art area.

Beside the desk I carefully curated a pile of documents, my 'later' pile, that I never, ever got to. My desk was messy too, although there was an order and, cliché, I could find anything because I knew where everything was. I had a whiteboard with current projects and progress figures, along with unrealistic exercise goals. Behold, my humanity.

That I didn't frame the review is what's important here.

Three years later, almost to the day, and while standing in the exact same spot, Tarquin, my literary agent, called.

'Double-Tee!'

'Don't call me that.'

'It's us. You and me, Double-Tee.'

'Why are you excited?'

'Can you tell?'

'Tarquin—'

'Okay, okay. Listen, do you know Francis Bacon?'

'The scientific method dude or the Screaming Popes guy?'

'What scientific method?'

'*Instauratio Magna?* Lord Bacon? None of this rings a bell?'

'I'm talking about the twentieth-century artist, Tade.'

'So Screaming Popes guy.'

'Yes.'

'What about him?'

'Well, he has people, right? The Francis Bacon people want to know if you'd be interested in writing a book, a novella, based on his works.'

'Not about him.'

'No. Not biographical. About his work.'

'And I can write what I like,' I said.

'Yes. Any genre you like.'

I could have said no. There was no pressing reason to take the job. My books were doing well; decent, even. I was in that mid-list sweet spot where I surfed the good side of the critics, the fans and the accountants. I was in the middle of writing a book, which my editor forked out the advance for, but seemed to hate. Then there were the screenplays that hadn't yet sent producers running for the hills. The work proceeded apace, no sign of a block anywhere, and reaped moderate but significant love during award season.

I could have said no.

And yet...

'It's interesting,' I said.

'Fabulous! I'll set up a meet.'

'Wait, what meet?'

'The Bacon folks will want to meet you, cast eyes on you to make sure you aren't a serial killer. Or that you *are* a serial killer, ha!'

'I said "interesting". I don't want to commit.'

'I'll set up the meetings. Bye. Bye!'

Excitable motherfucker.

Still, it couldn't be that difficult, could it? Besides, a lot of these things came up from time to time. About twice a week someone contacted Tarquin about me doing some work for a book or a television or radio show. Most of them didn't turn into anything more than expanding my circle of contacts. That's how it went.

I dropped my phone, pulled up my chair and continued with my novel-in-progress. By the time I'd finished one paragraph, I had forgotten all about Francis Bacon.

Trap, my son, came back from school and I spent the next two hours telling him to not do things, then the next half an hour telling him to do one thing, and when he fell asleep, I made love to my wife and slept a guilt-free sleep filled with wholesome, dreamless nothingness.

The next day, when I opened the door arriving from work, a post office slip unbalanced from the post box and fell to the mat. Shit. That usually meant a trip to the post office, seven miles round.

I waited till Saturday. Trap insisted on coming along. He was four and inquisitive, always drawing superheroes in his books and on the walls of the lounge. I got him one of those flexible whiteboard things to channel the artistic leanings, but he still scrawled on the paintjob and the sofa. What could I do? It's art.

'Where are we going?' he asked.

'To get a package from the post office.'

'Is it close to the toy shop?'

'No.' A lie. We would pass within five yards of the shop. The problem with Trap wasn't buying toys. It was the disappointment when the toy didn't do what the advert said it would. It stimulated a *Weltschmerz* of such a depth that it unsettled adults around him. I didn't want to deal with that.

The post office queue was modest and I gave the slip to Trap. The boy dutifully handed it to the post man. He scanned it, checked my driver's licence, and slouched out of the room.

He returned with a cardboard box, one foot by two, and the contractions of his forearm muscles told me that it was heavy. The return address said it was from Tarquin.

I thought the box contained author copies of my latest novel and took Trap to the toy shop to buy another toy that would trigger a melancholic wail.

The box was full of books about Francis Bacon. Seven hardcover tomes. One of them, my personal favourite, was entirely in German.

'Aren't they delightful?' said Tarquin over the phone. 'One of them is hard to find.'

'I didn't sign up for an art history degree,' I said.

'Oh, don't be a baby. You're a professional. You knew this job would mean research.'

'Yes, an online documentary, or something similar. Not... these.'

'Just take your time. There's no hard deadline just yet.'

As usual, we were not having the same conversation. Similar, but with enough adjacency to have separate meanings. I should have argued more, but Trap distracted me. Trap and I created a superhero duo called Jot and Tittle. They had shrinking powers, but only when they agreed with each other. Their powers didn't work when they argued, and since they were siblings, they argued all the time. Trap wanted to get to the next drawing and Tarquin was in the way.

I hung up without protesting hard enough, a mistake.

I'm systematic, anyone will tell you.

I get things done not because I'm smarter than other people, but because I'm organised and persistent. I'll keep at the task with some kind of evolving plan, and I'll do it long after most people would have quit and gone to the pub.

I set up a work schedule to get me through the research books. I would read three chapters a day, either from the same book or distributed across. On my whiteboard, I wrote the total number of chapters in all the books, and a daily tally.

One of them was a collection of photographs of Bacon's studio at 7 Reece Mews in London. I marked this down as a place I'd like to visit, but on the first page I learned it had been moved to Dublin. I loved Dublin. It wouldn't be a bad idea to go that far. I wanted to eyeball this mess, to lie on the ground and see it from an odd perspective, to feel the give of the floorboards and the slipperiness of the rope bannister. To smell the air and sniff the paint close up. It wasn't a good time to go. There was never a good time to visit a place where I've fallen in love on each visit, especially now that I was older and wiser. It was the accent and the attitude and the hair and the air off the Liffey.

The glossy photographs would have to do. My imagination was the next best thing. Besides, what could the smell possibly be other than mildew and turpentine, the earthy-chemical smell of paint, a hint of stale humanity?

Not going to lie, it was messy. 7 Reece Mews was a psychic compost heap, a record of the mind of a brilliant artist. On every flat surface I found paintbrushes in tea cups, soup cans, Libby's Orange Juice cans, Batchelors Butter Beans, Maxwell House coffee jars, mason jars and other containers too stained to identify. John Edwards, his last companion before death, said he never cleaned his brushes. The way the paintbrushes splayed out of the containers reminded me of those saprophytic plants that grow on trees.

I looked for some order, some organising principle, but all these photographs told me was that this person used whatever was at hand to create whatever he wanted.

I didn't know Francis Bacon at all. Nobody did.

I never called my own humble attic study messy again.

Bacon had a breadbasket with crumpled-up paper growing out of it like a head of beer. A biography of Karl Marx by Fritz J. Raddatz peeped between some papers. One wall held a circular brown stain with a stellate peeling pattern that seemed to turn it into a pie chart of obscure meaning. There were these scissors which, if they were any larger, would have to be called shears. The mirror in his living area was broken; the mirror in his studio area was speckled with black paint. A set of brush handles reaching out of a jar looked like a corpse's hand.

I noticed two things that often show up in his paintings. One was the light bulbs hanging from the ceiling with drawstrings. One of these was blue. The other was the ejaculatory splashes of white paint on the wall. I don't know if he employed other light sources, but the place seemed gloomy to me. I looked at each item in each photo, trying to absorb some essence of the painter from an image twice removed. I wanted a sense of the man's spirit.

Some of the items made sense as items used for improvisation. A cylinder of corduroy, cut from a trouser leg. A bent screwdriver. A pair of T-squares leaning on the wall. Dulux house paint, roller brushes. A cough mixture bottle holding Zeus knows what fluid.

The walls would have been at home in a crime scene photo if humans had blood of pink, blue, black and white. Cracked plaster, peeling paint, all saying Bacon did not give a fuck. The skylight was covered with brown paper and the general care was casual, desultory.

One hardcover book hidden among the paintbrushes and rollers was *Foundation of Modern* — nothing. Paper covered the rest of the title. When I got fatigued and my mind wandered I often speculated on the topic. Colour theory? Historiography? Biology? Jazz? There were a fair number of volumes whose titles I could not see, but this one was interrupted in the midst of telling me something about Francis. Ornithology, maybe?

I started a notebook for jotting down impressions. This, I assumed, would serve as my own compost heap. Reece Mews and everything else I had read about Bacon nudged me towards a singular personality, one I would have to open myself up to.

In order to write this, I must access and give full rein to my Id. Full subconscious release. Stab the superego to death.

After knowing him and his work, I'd move into the meat and bone of the assignment, which was writing a story dependent on that ferment. I had no story ideas at that time, but I was confident that if I immersed myself in his world a kernel of narrative would show up.

I was so naïve back then. I had no idea what I was dealing with. I thought it was a simple writing assignment that I could research, then shit out in a week or so, after which I'd return to normal transmission.

I was wrong, of course.

2

Trap woke up in the night and stumbled into our bedroom. He had this new thing where he would wake up screaming or crying, and for about two, three minutes he would squeeze his eyes shut, then he would open them, terrified, repeating the phrase 'who are you?' Soothing him usually took about ten minutes. He got it from his mother who, every six weeks, woke up in terror of a giant spider crawling across the ceiling. For Elise, it was always this specific thing, and she had done it since the first night she spent at my flat when we were dating. Gave me a fright with all her thrashing about. We weren't exactly dating, or rather we didn't realise we were until that particular night.

None of this would have been a problem were I not the lightest sleeper in the house. All this night-time activity meant I wasn't getting enough rest.

Trap was still going strong after fifteen minutes, so I opened every window and turned on all the lights, banishing the dark influences and the miasma to make the nightmares go away. I sang a song to him. I told him he was safe.

Twenty minutes, he was fine. Asleep again. I set him down beside his mother, closed the windows, turned out the light. I lay down to sleep, but my eyes would not even close. As an experienced insomniac, I knew how this went. Stay there too long and you'll never drop off. I got up, climbed the step ladder to my study in the attic.

I picked up the Bacon books with the intention of flipping through pages to get passive knowledge, an old study trick from medical school. When you're too tired to read, open the books and flip through, looking at diagrams, graphs and illustrations. Some knowledge will filter in and, with any luck, stay there.

I was looking to absorb a mood more than anything, but instead, I encountered Henrietta Moraes. Even now, after everything, my fingers hesitate to type these words. I saw the series of black-and-white photographs that John Deakin took of her. I live in the twenty-first century and I've seen nakedness, but I found Moraes disturbing. A woman comfortable naked and radiating effortless sexuality, she carelessly opened her legs to show her verdant pubic growth, spread across the bed, upside down with legs propped up on the wall, sitting, staring at the camera with a half-smile.

I'm stalling. The truth is on seeing the nude pictures of Henrietta Moraes I masturbated furiously and came in seconds. I only became aware of myself afterwards, breathing heavy, waiting for a wave of shame that never arrived. And there she was, not laughing, but smiling, telling me she knew the effect she had on men.

I'd like to say I put it out of my mind, cleaned up and went to bed, but that's not what happened. I tried reading something different, but my mind kept going back to her, and I got aroused again. I'm not fishing for absolution when I say my mind was not my own. A part of me thinks, typing this, that I'm going to delete it in the second draft, and that I don't have to worry about it. I was there for about forty-five minutes that night, and I wasn't researching.

I heard movement from downstairs and pulled up my pyjama bottoms too quickly out of guilt. I fell and hit my head on the edge of my desk on the way down. I didn't black out, but I was stunned, bright lights inside my eyelids. I stayed on the floor a bit, controlling my breathing, waiting for the throbbing pain to subside. I got up with care and navigated my way down the ladder.

My lust spent, I had a quick shower and went to sleep. I did not dream.

The next day, I got up like nothing happened, got ready, dropped Trap off at pre-school, went my way to the hospital, thinking that was the end of it.

I had a busy day, but I loved what I did, so it passed quickly. I can't talk about my work because of patient confidentiality. What I can tell you is I drank a smoothie for lunch and sat at my desk with my eyes closed, listening to music from my phone, trying to achieve a Zen state. This was what I usually did, and, combined with deep breathing exercises, it prepared me for the last third of my working day.

Only this time, Henrietta's face popped into my mind. Not her whole body, just her face, but my response was embarrassingly priapic. The tenting would be obvious to anyone who came into my office which, professionally, would be catastrophic. Nobody gossips like health workers. It takes our mind off the difficult things we have to do. I opened my door, looked up and down the corridor and, seeing nobody approaching, dashed into the men's room, led by the compass arrow behind my zip. I took a few seconds to stare down at my crotch, thinking of it as one does a disobedient child. I hadn't experienced this sort of thing since my teenage years, anarchic hormones trying to make sense of their role, telling me to mate and bring forth my own kind, telling me this is the best time with my cells spanking new, my DNA undamaged, my joints supple. Against that, social programming. Centuries of religion and convention bearing down on me, and some sense coming out of my testosterone-soaked brain about pregnancy and what used to be called venereal disease.

A girl taught me to masturbate. I used to have wet dreams like everybody else, but they weren't linked to what I would later call sex at all. I'd have fragmentary dreams of longing without knowing what I was longing for, then a weird sensation and voila I would have to clean my sheets. She was my puppy-love girlfriend, though. She was a lot more experienced than me, might have been a year or two older, which is like ten years in wisdom. We kissed mostly. Rubbed against each other. This went on for a while, but I started getting erections and one day she stroked me from the outside of my shorts. Boom. An entirely new sensation and a new frontier in laundry.

I was still naïve in a psycho-sexual way, and it took me a long time to realise I could touch myself, and that was only after we broke up. I didn't even link it to pornography. Back then, in Lagos, they sold comics and porn from the same outlet, which tells you everything you need to know about societal attitudes to comics, I guess. But not really, because you could buy comics elsewhere, and I think they used the comics to transport the porn instead of the brown paper bags that came later. I knew porn was naked people doing weird stuff to each other, but I didn't link it to any of my hidden activities. I was there for the comics, but sometimes a glossy magazine would slip between my Marvel issues. I would look through them. Nobody seemed to be having any fun, faces in contortion. A few of the faces looked bored, which I didn't understand until much later. As it stood, I found the photos completely unarousing.

This all came back to my mind, compressed, Proust style, while I stood in that bathroom.

None of it helped me with my Henrietta problem.

I took matters into my own hands.

I achieved little that day. I didn't trust myself to be with people because Henrietta was right there, grinning. Any pleasure I might have derived from the whole mess quickly dissipated. It hurt to walk; it hurt to sit down; it hurt to stand up fully. I found relief only in a hunched posture, like Quasimodo. I wondered if I should go to Accident and Emergency. Prolonged erections can be harmful and could indicate blood problems. But I couldn't do that because my colleagues were there. My job took me to the general hospital at least twice a week to give opinions on people who turned up with mental distress. How would I live it down? They'd think I took Viagra or something. My protestations would make it worse. Any time I had to visit A&E after that I'd see smirks in everyone, even if they were not present.

There was a second problem: the treatment. In extreme cases you have to drain blood. Yes, I've seen it done, and it's about as much fun as it sounds.

That wasn't the worst thing for me. Sickle cell disease can cause priapism and I carried the trait. In my panicked state, I wondered if I had been misdiagnosed all those years back.

West Africans tend to find out their sickle cell status early in life. There are three genotypes: AA, with no trait; AS, carrier state; and SS, disease. It's not that simple, and there are other variants, each with their own funky letter. We've only been carriers for one generation, thanks to my mother. My dad liked to point that out from time to time when he was feeling belligerent. Because we're carriers, in my family children are told early not to marry for love, or at least only marry for love someone who doesn't have the sickle cell trait. Yes, it's heteronormative. No, adoption isn't even hinted at. Yes, it's a heavy trip to lay on a pre-teen. What can I say? Sickle cell anaemia kills people.

I briefly contemplated driving to a different town.

I begged off work and went home. Alone, I stripped off, took a shower, drank a litre of water, waited.

I checked my medical textbooks and, ignoring causes like leukaemia and thalassaemia, I found something else to try.

I put on the loosest shorts I could find, donned my boxing gloves, and worked on the punching bag I had set up in the backyard.

Henrietta laughed, but I kept going. Sweating, exhausted from the workout and anxiety, the hardness finally abated.

When Trap got back, I cooked spaghetti, which he said he wanted, but subsequently refused to eat because the bolognaise had cloves in it. Trap is a picky eater. He won't eat beans. He won't eat bread if it has seeds in it. He doesn't like mixed textures, so he'll eat yogurt, but not if it has bits of fruit in it. He'll eat fruit, but not a fruit salad. He won't even eat strawberries if they've touched any other fruit. He likes bananas, but he has exacting standards for what constitutes an edible one. A single blemish disqualifies. Any of those white strings that stick to bananas makes it verboten. He'll also baulk if the banana is not smoothly separated from the peel.

I'm making it sound like he was difficult to feed. He wasn't. If anything, I found his foibles amusing, though he was dead serious.

I used Trap as a human shield that day. We were working on a picture book together. I was busy with my son, then I had writing to do. I had no time to cuddle my wife.

I didn't sleep that night; too afraid. I feared any morning wood, but all was calm. I looked down there and the skin was peeling off. I showered with care and avoided moisturising because I feared what the rubbing would do.

I got through the day without acting like a pervert.

Henrietta was nowhere.

I went to my GP to ask for some blood tests, giving a fabricated history of dizziness and headaches, which, to be fair, I still had from banging my head. I mentioned nothing of my pelvic difficulties. My doctor's a genteel and gentle older Asian woman. She didn't need to hear a nasty story like mine, and even if she wanted to hear it, I wasn't going to tell. I could just imagine what would happen to those kind eyes in every subsequent visit. *Of course I'm not judging you, but I'm judging you.*

Elise noticed the plaster on the inside of my elbow while we ate dinner.

She jabbed her fork in the air between us and said, 'When you get a social disease it's polite to tell your wife.'

'Hmm? Oh, this. I went to the GP,' I said.

'Right.'

'I was dizzy. I wanted to be sure I'm not getting anaemia from my sickle cell.'

'You don't have sickle cell,' she said, forking asparagus into her mouth.

'I do.'

'You don't. You have sickle cell trait, which, thanks for passing that to our son, by the way.'

'Fine. I have the trait.'

'Nobody gets anaemia from the trait, Tade.'

This was true. She knew more about it than most people because she'd been on a research binge ever since I told her, about a week before our wedding. She did not take it badly, but she probably would have appreciated being told earlier, like before I proposed.

'But sometimes you can get haematuria and rhabdomyolysis,' I said.

'Exercise-induced sudden death, bacteriuria, papillary necrosis… I know. They're rare,' said Elise.

'Why are we talking about this?' I asked.

'I don't know. You went for a test? You doth protest too much, methinks.'

'You want to call the GP?'

'Jesus, I'm kidding,' she said.

I got up and retreated to the kitchen.

In the study, later, I tried to find the soul of Francis Bacon and I could not. I struggled to find a way in. I read that he had asthma, and in his papers were instruction manuals for inhalers. I dropped downstairs to find my own Ventolin inhaler. I hadn't needed it in years. I had some low-grade allergies that at times caused me to wheeze. The inhaler, on examination, had expired three years prior. I shook it and sprayed it, inhaling. There's a trick to it that even children master quickly, but that I've never quite got the hang of. Bitter at the back of the throat, like cocaine.

I licked the plastic. I can't tell you why.

It had no taste.

3

I was wandering around Marylebone, looking for a place called *Rebecca's* to meet the Bacon people. I'd never been comfortable in this area in the daytime. At night, inebriated, I could find any eating or drinking joint in inner London. In the daytime, sober, it seemed like alien territory, and it oppressed me with unfamiliarity. I didn't know why; it wasn't like the street names had changed.

Rebecca's was somewhere in the scalene triangle between Goodge Street, Oxford Street and Bond Street underground stations. I was early, so I leisurely went down blind alleys and walked past the backs of restaurants where staff scanned me with bored eyes. Those eyes told me they'd given up on whatever the dream was. A constant fear of mine was to see those eyes in the mirror one day.

Nobody tried to sell me anything or win me over to a cause during this perambulation, which was unusual for me. I have the kind of face that invites solicitation.

I found *Rebecca's*. It was narrow, and the sign was in cursive. One of those joints that you had to know about to get to, I guessed. They didn't want anybody off the street, which was fine by me.

I was thirty minutes early and they sat me near the window. I didn't quite know what the meeting was about. This was one of the more confusing parts of being a writer, especially a gun-for-hire. People who were interested in giving you gigs wanted to meet you, but there would be no agenda. You just sat and talked, conversational, but with an undercurrent of evaluation. They would have seen your CV, they'd be generally happy with the work, but they wanted to know if you were an arsehole, because there's nothing worse than locking yourself into a one-year contract with someone nobody wants to work with.

Two of them arrived on time, Audrey and Deidre. Audrey was a willowy white woman who looked like a strong wind would blow her away, but in point of fact had a steely handshake. Deidre was darker, and I'd guess she had some Asian in her. My height, sharp brown eyes. Both of them smelled fantastic; you tended to notice that kind of thing after a morning on the tube with commuters.

'We're very excited about this project,' said Audrey.

'Very,' said Deidre.

'So am I,' I said. To be polite.

'I have more source material for you,' said Audrey. She dumped three hardcover books on the tiny breakfast table.

'So do I,' said Deidre. She dumped her pile of books.

'Great. I can't wait to get into them,' I said, with enthusiasm I did not feel. I was only halfway through the books Tarquin had sent me.

I made a neat tower of the books and one of them slid to the floor. It opened to a chaste headshot of Henrietta.

And I made for the toilets.

Here we go again.

Later, Tarquin said they thought I was interesting and odd, like some kind of eccentric genius. 'They're delighted. They think you're mad.'

'And that's a good thing?' I asked.

'In everything you've read about Bacon, is any of it conventional? This is exactly the kind of weird shit they want. Speaking of shit, did you have diarrhoea?'

I looked at where I was: the cramped toilet of a National Rail train being suffused by the urine fumes of a thousand strangers, afraid to be at my seat in case Henrietta got me in trouble.

'Yes, I have diarrhoea,' I said.

'Next time they're going to need a bit more from you, old chap. You know, some idea of the plot of your novella.'

'Sure. Easy.'

Just as soon as I exorcised the succubus.

I decided this problem was best viewed as an obsessive-compulsive issue and maybe I could use the same treatment methods to resolve it. When it comes to thoughts and behaviour it's often unhelpful to try not to think of something, in my case Henrietta Moraes. Trying in that way just makes you think of the thing more. The best strategy is to replace the ruminations with an obsession of your own design. Thoughts can be crafted.

First, I started a coded thought diary. The last thing I wanted was for Elise to find my wank journal. I don't know what would have been worse: her finding it, or her finding out that I was defiling myself because of a woman who died in 1999. Elise and I are okay, not fantastic, and that middle-ground kind of marriage is predicated on predictability, persistence and probity, rather than mad your-love-will-kill-me passion. I've had the other kind. It burns out and, really, you want to be in another county when the reactor goes critical.

I called the journal *Regarding Henry* and drew up columns for the dates and times I thought of Henrietta and when I pleasured myself as a result. I had to interrupt the process twice. This was the odd thing. I had never been this red-blooded. I think Elise would be shocked, then surprised, then curious as to why this situation seemed able to stoke me to stroking.

I spent a week recording in *Regarding Henry*.

I bought a twelve-ounce beef steak and slapped it on my desk in the attic. I stared at it, following the marbling with my eyes. I thought of Henrietta and stared at the meat. I let it rot, associating Henrietta with the decomposition, down to the olfactory assault, and stared at it.

The meat darkened, the fat slimed on to the wood, maggots burst free and explored, throbbing about like mini-penises, themselves stilling and darkening as they finished their life-cycle. I watched this daily and it became the highlight of my day so that the rot fixed in my mind as a rapid event, while everything else about that fortnight seemed sped up and irrelevant. I can't tell you what happened in the rest of my life at that time. I know Elise thought we had a dead rat and commanded me to contact exterminators. I know she said the smell was coming from the attic, but we have a rule about nobody going up into my study.

It got so whenever I had a flash of Henrietta's face, I thought of rotting meat and the erection subsided immediately.

Easy.

Fuck you, Moraes. Get out of my head with your easy sensuality. My kung fu is powerful.

I could get back to my life and find a way into this novella.

To celebrate my newfound control, I bought some wine that Elise liked and cooked a fancy dinner; fancy for me, that is. Fish. I didn't think I'd be eating meat for a few months. I also lit scented candles and got rid of the offspring.

'This is a surprise,' said Elise. 'You've been distracted lately.'

'I know. I'm sorry. This book is irritating me. It's the last time I'm doing commissioned work, I promise.'

I left out the weird psychosexual journey the research had triggered in me.

I was attentive, I showed off, I pretended to know about the wine even though I had spent the last few days memorising facts about this specific bottle. A week later and all I'd be able to say was white wine goes with fish and can be chilled.

We started kissing before the meal ended. The wine bottle followed us up the stairs, into our room. We shed clothes like snakes shed skin, peeling them off by rubbing against each other.

I should have known where this was going to go.

As soon as we were on the bed, I closed my eyes and got a flash of Henrietta and, as per my programming, a prolonged burst of rotting meat.

Almost on cue, Elise said, 'What's wrong?'

That was the end of the night's activity.

I blamed everything from the vintage of the wine to overwork. Elise nodded that way women do at times like this. It's always a knife edge, non-committal, not quite blaming you, but not absolving you either. There's a vulnerability, of course, that idea that maybe they're just not attractive enough, or you don't like them enough.

In the gloom, I could swear there was a third person in the room with us and laughing at me, at my hubris, at my inability to rise.

Fucking Henrietta

I fell asleep by mistake and woke up groggy, avoiding eye contact with Elise.

The next day was a Saturday and I spent it hiding, up in the study which was still imbued with a faint rotting meat smell. Elise and

Trap were out for the day, a garden centre or something similar. I was glad to have the house all to myself.

I cooked brown rice, made fish stew to go with it, ate, washed it down with warm white wine left from the night before.

Maybe I just didn't want the assignment. It was a departure from what I had always done, except was it? I hadn't done any work based on or derived from another person before, true. But they said I could go where I wanted with it. This should have been freedom. They were paying for literary freedom.

By then, my diary looked like a knock-off *Portnoy's Complaint*. I was alarmed to find I had dispensed with the code and had written all my perversions in plain English. I burnt it in the backyard and ground the ashes into powder. I felt furtive, like I was getting rid of a corpse, and when I looked around, I saw the windows of my neighbours. I imagined them glued to the glass, watching me, judging me and considering calling the police or social services or something.

I set up an online poker app on my phone because I didn't know gambling and it was one of the pillars of Bacon's life. I'd gambled before, but sporadically, as entertainment. Baccarat, roulette, that sort of thing. The poker could go on in the background. I'd check later to be sure it didn't get out of hand and to see if I could learn something.

Back in the house, I looked at some Bacon reproductions, confident that the inspiration for my story would lie in there. I remember canine teeth, but nothing more of that day.

Time ticked away and I hadn't started. I didn't even have a direction. The usual trick at times like this is to start and see where the words take me. The words didn't have to be good, clear, or pretty. They only had to take me away from the blank page. When people talk of writer's block, I think of sculpture. The block is raw material to chip away at until the true form is revealed. So I create a block of text and prune until I see structure.

But this was Francis Bacon, right? He was never going to be typical, never going to be routine.

I gave up that particular day at midnight.

Idle, I thought of other parts of the world where it wasn't midnight, and meridians and the king of Tonga or Fiji who changed timezone by edict on the event of the new millennium. What a power to have. The ability to determine time.

I command time to move backwards.

I command it to be 1953 so I can talk to this slippery motherfucker myself.

I fell asleep before I could determine if spacetime had obeyed my command, and by the time I woke up I was in my own day and age.

Pity.

4

I had been staring at the Bacon books for hours. Morning light streamed in with improbable cheer. I looked out of the attic's skylight and saw the world as wet, layered not with dew, but the shower that fell just before dawn. The leaves on the trees, the sheds in the allotment, the asphalt, they all looked new, full of promise.

My pen poised over my notebook; my mind barren.

Not entirely true. My mind was fertile with dozens of other projects which I scribbled down ferociously. Not that I didn't want them, I just didn't want them then.

Frustrated, I pushed away from my desk. I decided to approach in the oblique, not at Bacon, but at his inspiration. I had Eadweard Muybridge's *The Human Figure in Motion* on my shelf, and I knew it was on Bacon's radar. I opened a random page, and it turned out on Plate 57: Men Boxing.

The young men in the photos weren't truly fighting, and they had open palms; a staged slap-fight, really. Twelve photos. Blocking, slipping, weaving, ducking.

This was much better. Violence was something I knew intimately: the sexual kind; the random, unexpected kind; the disciplined, martial variety, and everything in between.

I come from violence.

We arrive at the matter of my mother.

The fact is, I was an unwanted child. I had to prove my worth over time, but in proving it, realised that I shouldn't have to.

My parents' marriage was a sham, based on false pretences from the very start. My mother only pretended to love my father. She needed him to transport her from Nigeria to London where her true love lived. Her plan was to seduce this rich dude, my dad, that is, follow him to London, then disappear into the loving arms of her beau. Which she did, but without counting on my father's tenacity. He found her and, according to him, dragged her back to the marital home five times.

That fifth time, though. Yeah, that was the beginning of my psychological life.

My mother and her lover had called it quits and she had moved into a shelter or some kind of home. My father went there, coaxed her out because men were not allowed, and raped her in the back of a truck. This was in full view of the Wimbledon public. People came to help and apparently he kept shouting, 'She's my wife! She's my wife!' or whatever the fuck.

Reader, that's where I came into the picture. From this sexual assault, this rape, I was conceived.

Pregnant, my mother returned to my father's house, which began a tumultuous nine months, during which my father was physically and emotionally abusive. Police were involved on at least one occasion – I've seen the report. One time, when she was about seven months along, my mother was found unconscious in a pool of blood.

Are you disgusted yet?

As soon as I was born, my mother hated my fucking face because I looked like my father. I mean, I don't blame her for this given the horrific time she had, but I didn't do anything to deserve being the object of her hatred.

Not a great start to life, you have to admit.

Plus, stress hormones from the mother definitely affect the baby.

Plus, I'm guessing each time my mother looked at me she had a flashback to rape and physical violence.

The first violence I experienced outside television and outside the womb was from my stepfather. The TV part is important because as a child I never really thought violence was real, that killing was real. And when I thought it might be real, I didn't know whether it hurt and if it did hurt, how much. I'd seen people in films punch other people to unconsciousness with one blow and no blood, so, naturally, I thought if you swung your fist at someone, they would fall asleep. I was a weird, quiet kid. I hadn't got into any playground fights by then.

Up until that time my stepfather George had been blustery, yelling and the like, and maybe he had scuffed me once or twice, but nothing that I remember. One day, when I was nine, I crossed the living room. He was on the sofa watching television, drinking a beer, a lit cigarette unspooling a line of blue smoke to the ceiling where a lazy fan dispersed it.

As I passed him, his leg lashed out like a striking scorpion, hitting me in the flank and hurling me across the room. Only the screen doors stopped me from rolling out to the balcony. If you've ever been hit in the gut you know it's a different kind of pain from everywhere else. It spreads everywhere in an instant. Later, in medical school, I found out this is due to the tangle of nerves called the coeliac plexus. The abdomen has an apron of fat called the omentum, and fat is liquid at body temperature. Liquid transmits force uniformly in a sealed container, called Pascal's Law, the basis of hydraulics. The abdomen is a sealed container. You hit someone in the gut, the force is transmitted rapidly and equally to the coeliac plexus. If the strike is forceful enough, the diaphragm is pushed upwards, and you're out of breath.

Oh, and the coeliac plexus is what is commonly and mistakenly called the solar plexus. Alas, pulp writers, there is no solar plexus.

I didn't know any of this when I was nine. I just knew I'd been shoved like a tenpin and was in pain like I had never known. The surprise of the unexpected was almost as bad as the pain, but that wasn't the worst part. The worst part was his face.

When you hit a child, he tries to understand the reason, what he's done wrong, where the mistake was, what to avoid next time.

George was blank, no emotion, no yelling, no anger, no drunkenness, just... smooth features. I can't even say he was looking at me at all. For a moment, and for some days after, I even wondered if I had imagined the whole thing. This uncertainty only lasted until he did it again.

This changed my life. My house became an obstacle course where I had to avoid George at all costs. I spent a lot of time outside, and when I was home I tried to be in the company of other people because the dude only hit me when I was alone. But, like I said, I was a strange boy and nobody wanted to hang out with me. I also enjoyed being alone so seeking others went against my natural inclination.

It went on. I did not bruise. I'm black, and he was smart enough to hit me where it wouldn't show even if it could. You're wondering where my mother was. Let's just say she and I didn't have the kind of relationship where I could open up to her. When I did tell her, years later, she did not believe me, or chose to say she didn't.

I found indirect ways of telling. I said I had a belly ache and chest pains, which were true sensations. I just didn't say where they were coming from. I had ultrasounds and x-rays and trips to the doctor, none of which revealed anything. I had hoped something would show up and the doctor would say, 'This boy is being beaten up. Stop immediately!' but that never happened.

Obviously, I had to run away.

The first time I had no real plan except to leave. I slipped out at four pm and started walking. It seemed like hours, but it always does to children. Left my street, my area, into some woods. As I walked through the trees it started to get dark and I was too scared to go back the way I came in case it took too long, and forward because I didn't know how much longer it would be before I got out.

Well. Stupid. There was no end. I mean, yes, there was, but not an end that a nine-year-old boy could reach on foot. Exhausted, I found a patch of grass and lay down, curled up in the same way I did when George beat me. Cold and wet, living things crawled underneath me so I kept moving. The tiredness must have taken me, because I woke up with people standing over me.

They took me home. My cover story was that I got lost, which was true in a way. I got lost while running away.

The second time I ran away was a year later. At ten I was all grown up and wiser. I took supplies this time, for example. I also scouted the route by skipping school a few times. I realised that the best way to do this would be to pretend to go to school, change clothes, get my stash of food, and keep going. I could make good time before they even realised I was gone. I had not a single mitigating thought, no reason to stay. My mother... yes, maybe, we'll get to her later.

My plan was to go by the railyard and sleep in a large concrete pipe, then set off again. I did get to the pipe, but my supplies were gone. Some homeless person must have found them, I don't know. I contemplated just going on the lam, like an outlaw, hunted by the forces of child abuse, but I was tired. I went home late and I got a kicking.

Since the beatings continued, and I didn't see how I could run away, logic dictated that I would kill myself. I fantasised about stabbing myself in the gut and being found bleeding to death. It was important that they found me alive, not going cold. I wanted to see the looks on their faces when they realised what they had done to me. Which is weird logic, but don't fucking beat your children and you won't have to face it. In fact, don't have children, you wankers. Work out your aggression on a punching bag.

I say that, but what I'm hiding is that my father, my biological father, was also violent. My mother had a thing for abusive, controlling men, I guess.

I never actually attempted to kill myself. I did flirt with a knife one afternoon, but never followed through. Later, when I was an adult and life became too interesting, I acquired some insulin and a syringe with the intention of putting myself into a fatal coma if nothing worked out. I kept that in the fridge all the time until the day Elise found it and, being the common-sense person she was, threw it out.

5

None of my usual literary tricks worked.

Elise saw that the project was driving me to distraction and said, 'You are mistaken. Francis Bacon is not the assignment. You don't need to learn the soul of the man if you're not writing his biography.'

She wasn't wrong. I found Bacon as silent now as when I started. He was unknowable, his mysteries eluding me more and more as my research intensified.

I wrote a trashy vampire story to loosen up the words. It only loosened vampire words. I sedated myself to avoid Henrietta and slept like a dead man. In the morning I had an idea, not the literary kind, but the type to shine the light of optimism on endeavours. Everything would be all right.

I took a train to Brixton.

A colleague of mine once got a flat a few yards from Brixton tube station; this was in the late 90s. She was mugged twice on the same night on her way home. She never returned. I was mugged when I was twelve or thirteen, although it was without violence. In the same area my younger brother was set upon by four muggers and had to spend time in hospital after being robbed. He fought back, too stupid to surrender. In the face of unfavourable odds, as Sun Tzu never wrote, get the fuck out of there.

But those are the worst experiences. I'd still rather live there or Stockwell, all a mile from where I was born, and South London is the only place I truly feel at home. What can I tell you? First kisses mean something.

Out of the train and I started to feel energised; hometown invigoration. I started to have flashbacks of loud jungle and drum and bass, just walking by old record shops. I aimed myself at Brixton Market, a place where you can buy everything. I wasn't buying, well, I wasn't buying commodities. I was in the market for a service.

Just before I turned into the aisle I wanted, I got sudden gooseflesh, like the International Space Station had passed over my birth spot.

Dotun was there, selling knock-off DVDs. Not Blu-ray, DVDs. He specialised in mindless action flicks on the face of it, but his under-the-counter stuff was DVD rips from streaming porn sites (*not now, Henrietta*). Yes, there were a lot of older folk who did not stream their porn, and Dotun supplied them all.

But that wasn't why I was there.

'Oh, boy, wey you, na?' I said.

'Doktor Tade! Which ones?'

We shook hands and hugged.

'What can I do for you, sir? Why are you in my office?'

I hummed a few bars of a song.

Dotun looked at his watch. 'Give me ten minutes.' Which in Nigeriaspeak means an hour.

While waiting I browsed a second-hand bookshop that had a narrow frontage, but seemed excavated deep inside like those places in Amsterdam. I remembered a girlfriend of mine lived close by, and I had a flashback to neuron-ripping sex and arguments about Proust. I could not remember her face. Brief encounters.

The song I hummed to Dotun was 'Babalawo mo wa Bebe',

which, loosely, means 'I need your help, priest'.

I better give you a crash course on Yoruba cosmology before we get to the next bit.

There's heaven and there's Earth, but no hell. God is in heaven, and he sent a whole bunch of supernatural folks to Earth. One of those is Orunmila, his son and the god of order; another is Eshu, god of chaos. Ifá divination gets input from both. Babalawo are the ones who perform the divination.

Dotun is a babalawo.

Now you are an expert.

Later, in his flat, his narrow and dilapidated place, he produced a flat dish and uncorked a bottle. He poured sea sand into the dish.

He looked up. 'Who do you want to enquire about?'

'Francis,' I said.

'Mother's name?'

'Christina. Winnie.'

'Which is it?'

'Winnie.'

Dotun's forehead creased.

'What's the matter?' I said, fearful that he'd discovered Henrietta.

'He's white?'

'Yes.'

Dotun sucked his teeth, chiding me. 'Go out and get me sand. This sand is from Lagos. Get some sand from this land, where white blood has been shed.'

I used to own a flat in Potters Bar. I liked it, although I was never able to convince any woman to come live there with me. After I sold it, I kept dreaming of owning it. I still do. The dreams vary, but the universal theme is of me forgetting that I live there or ought to be living there or ought to visit. In the dream I usually take a desperate trip to the property and find squatters or tenants or encroachments by people who just seem weird, but my flat would be empty, no furnishings, no drapes, no nothing. I have this dream every few months, like an anxiety dream.

I had it on the train on the way to Brixton, but in dreamworld the building had just been demolished, rubble in the process of being cleared away by heavy machinery. All that remained was sand.

This was not creepy at all.

Me, a grown man, wandering around Brixton playgrounds, looking for soil from sandpits. Luckily, it was a school day and nobody but the most hardcore of truants were out. I did scrape together enough – using a cotton bud container from Boots – and I took it back to Dotun without getting myself on the sex offenders register.

Dotun had a thing, a lesion, on his upper lip. He wouldn't get it looked at because he believed it gave him a clearer connection to the spirit world. 'You don't shave Samson's hair,' he once told me.

I focused on it while waiting. It looked like a raisin sunk into his skin and mortared in place.

Dotun dropped his hands. 'He's not there.'

'What do you mean?' I asked.

'There's nobody there. Nobody's answering.'

Worth a try. I didn't know what I had expected. I didn't fully believe in Ifa, but I didn't disbelieve either. I had seen some weird things in my time. Still. Maybe white people's spirits didn't work in the same way. They did have that self-flagellating concept of hell. What if Bacon's spirit thought he ought to be punished? Like he did with his body.

Wait.

'Check for Jessie Lightfoot. Jessie.'

'What's his mother's name?' asked Dotun, smoothing the sand.

'Her. And I don't know. Just look. Jessie was a medium of sorts.'

Dotun pressed and stroked the sand, pursed his lips and shook his head.

'Sorry, bruv.'

I gave him a fifty.

'You want to talk to your dad?'

'Fuck, no. I'll be in touch.' I stood.

'Where are you going? I'm about to cook.'

'Why didn't you say so?'

On the way home, on the train, jostled by its movement into the person on my right and my left. The person in front of me was eating a cornish pasty that I'm sure he got from the kiosk at the station. My belly was full of Dotun's food, but the aroma from the pasty made my mouth water. I felt an intense urge to leap up, snatch the snack and bite into it. I wasn't hungry, so I couldn't understand the want. I stood, moved to another carriage. What was going on?

I found a seat, sat down and closed my eyes.

You didn't go to a medium or psychic for information. At least, that wasn't how I understood it. You went to witches and clevermen to speak to your own subconscious, to shake something loose.

A writer's work is mining the subconscious, the deep well where all of life experience and learning mixes together and sprouts something new, and if you do it right, it feels original to readers, the Holy Grail of art. It can only be original if it is a true reflection of the deep mind of the artist, and that requires honesty whether you're writing about robots or vampires or suburban life.

If Dotun had found nothing, heard nothing, did that mean my subconscious was empty?

Once, years ago, I had eighteen months of psycho-analytic therapy. What I remember the most is how the psychotherapist found me frustrating. I didn't notice this myself, but she said so in one of her interpretation sessions, where she theorised about our journey so far, and offered hypotheses.

'You're very well defended,' she had said. 'You've set up shields in almost every aspect of your life and you feel no psychic pain. You have a moat, a castle, and a squad of knights. You sit in this impregnable space, and you're smug. Don't be. You're young. It'll work for a decade, two at most. Then it'll come crumbling down.'

'I think you're just cynical,' I said.

'No. I'm experienced and I am very good at my job.'

She was right. Eleven years later, I nearly destroyed my life by being stupid. I came back from the brink by focusing on something she told me to look out for, on an unconscious need to self-sabotage.

It turns out when you have an unstable childhood, one of the reactions is to expect instability at all times so that when things are going relatively well, you're waiting for the other shoe to drop, and if that shoe takes too long, why, you have to do something to help it fall. Drop that fucker yourself. It'll be chaos, but chaos is familiar: chaos is where you live. You might be suffering, but you're used to that, and life goes on.

My eyes flicked open as I was seized with the certainty that I had missed my stop. I hadn't, but I felt like I was being watched. There were only two other people in the carriage at this time, well spaced out. One was knitting, while the other seemed engrossed in a glossy while chewing the cud. I stared at the cover of the glossy, looking for cracks in the narrative the cover stories told. Looking for a discreet hole through which the reader might be observing me. It sounds silly now and it felt silly then, but I promised myself I would write everything. There was no hole because it was not a 1940s detective story. I left the train at the next stop all the same.

I still felt observed, so I walked all the way home, with my phone in my chest pocket, camera facing outward, set on record.

I got home, slammed the front door shut, rushed from the hall to the living room and parted the blinds a crack, just a sliver to see the road. Nothing. Nobody. A hammer kept up a rhythmic banging for a few seconds, then stopped.

I went up to the bathroom and soaked my feet in warm water while going over the footage on my phone. When the film ended, I started again, just in case I had missed something. And again. And again. I shivered, and realised that the water had gone cold while I was checking my phone. My feet had those prune water wrinkles and for a second, I didn't recognise them as my own.

I took a hot shower to warm up and reset myself.

I didn't have anyone to call. I couldn't call Elise because I didn't find talking to her comforting. It just wasn't the kind of relationship we had. She didn't handle problems well. They brought out a selfish side to her and she would panic and make it worse by talking about the problems that her perspective of my problem would bring to her. It was best not to tell her anything unless it had a specific connection to her.

I did what I always do: I went up into the attic to read. I climbed up in my housecoat, which was unwise, but I was tired and lonely.

I sat down and read Blake for an hour or so. I can't remember what it was, but I know there were illustrations with that subversive ecclesiastical energy that Blake always brought.

I yawned, looked up, and there, in the corner, stood a woman in Coke-bottle glasses, still, staring right at me.

'Uh...' I said.

I dropped Blake and rocked backwards in the chair.

She was slight and grey, by which I mean all the colours around her were muted, a kind of blending. Her eyes were the main thing, fixed, powerful, and with a suppressed monomania.

Dotun hadn't failed.

This was Jessie Lightfoot.

Even if you never had a nanny, you'd be able to imagine what a nanny could do. Granted, not every nanny could be practically perfect in every way like the supercalifragilisticexpialidocious Mary Poppins, or that other Julie Andrews alter ego, but you can imagine the basics: dress children up, wipe their arses, soothe them when they cry, keep them away from the parents when the parents don't want to see their offspring, which tends to be quite often, strangely. A nanny teaches everything from manners to ABCs, and if you're thinking of a kind of surrogate mother, you'd be right.

We had a nanny, my siblings and I. Her husband, Roland, was responsible for my earliest memory, which is holding on tight to his back while he gave me a ride on his motorbike. I was like three, man. You'd never get away with that these days. I can't remember much about Janet, but I do know that about ten, fifteen years ago she got in trouble and threatened to blow up a tower block with two jerry cans of petrol as a dramatic way of killing herself. I kid you not. She wasn't even arrested. My mother called the police and they confiscated the petrol.

Immediately after they were gone, she called my mother and said they hadn't found all of her stash, and that she was going to self-immolate. So not Mary Poppins, then.

But let's get back to Jessie Lightfoot.

Did your nanny do the basic childcare stuff, then move in with you as an adult, help you score illicit drugs, sleep on the kitchen table, go out with you to commit petty crime to fund your necessities, your drug habit? Was your nanny your pimp when you indulged in a spot of prostitution? Was she your medium? Did she control access to you while being the surrogate parent you needed when your biological mother was a bit casual about the whole thing? That, I understood, was who Jessie Lightfoot was to Francis Bacon.

Nanny Lightfoot organised illegal gambling in Bacon's residence and charged a generous tip when guests needed to use the loo. There is a racehorse named after her right now. I can see her knitting in the corner of the room, glancing over the 'gentleman's companion' respondents' letters, deciding who Bacon would offer services to while being rabidly homophobic herself. She apparently believed in capital punishment for sodomy, among other things. I'm told she thought the Duchess of Windsor should be the first to be hanged, drawn and quartered at Marble Arch. Lightfoot was loyal to Bacon and Bacon was loyal to Lightfoot.

Jessie Lightfoot died in 1951, sending Francis Bacon off on a brief spiral of instability.

And she was in my fucking study.

You invited her.

I blinked, closed my eyes for sixty seconds and opened them again. I pinched myself (why do we do that? Does it ever work in dreams? Has anybody ever been able to wake themselves up from a dream that way?). None of this made Lightfoot disappear.

I was scared, of course, seeing anything that wasn't there. But seeing a person, and that person being Lightfoot, somehow made it worse. When it came to Bacon, Lightfoot had no flex. I didn't know if she could harm me, I didn't know if her presence was meant to chastise me for what I was doing, I didn't know if I should be reacting to her or ignoring her. I felt unprepared for this encounter. I liked to be prepared. I liked instructions, manuals, briefings. This left me at sea.

It was different from Henrietta. Moraes was more my own projection, a perverse extrapolation from a Deakin image, very little to do with the actual person, more to do with my own depravity. Lightfoot, on the other hand, seemed to have an agenda.

She stood there, breathing, taking up psychic space, her mouth a thin line.

'What do you want?'

No answer.

No matter. I scrambled down the attic, almost tripping over the housecoat belt. I managed to get down without falling to my death. I stripped it off and hurled it from me. Naked, I went to the bedroom and closed the door. Lightfoot was waiting for me, in a corner, still. Why was she staring? I'd read that in life she was practically blind.

I closed my eyes. Henrietta was there.

'What?'

I phased through the Henrietta-rotten-meat cycle, but it was too little aversion too late. Maybe being naked didn't help the situation. This is one of those times where, because of the shame, my fingers slow down in the typing of this account and outright stop. Right there, under the gaze of Jessie Lightfoot, I pleasured myself, if one can call it that. She did not react. I didn't imagine she would show or feel disgust. She'd seen far, far worse perversions and been an accomplice to as many.

The bedroom carpet needed work before Elise came home.

Those two were in my head now: Lightfoot when my eyes were open, Henrietta when they were closed. The worst part of this was the rotting meat, which persisted without curbing my arousal. On some occasions it worked the other way around, as in, I'd smell rotting meat, see it, then get aroused, then see Henrietta. Any meat could set it off.

Lightfoot, meanwhile, was everywhere. Home, work, on the cycle path, in the car, in the gents. No matter how cramped the space was, Lightfoot would be there staring, silent.

I started to lose my appetite because putrefaction has never quite done it for me as a spice.

When I was with people I made a concerted effort to ignore Lightfoot, but, when alone in the attic, I took to speaking to her.

'Where's Francis? Why are you here? What do you want? Can you just fuck off now? I have work to do. FUCK. OFF.'

Not even a ripple on the blankness of her expression.

Not that I didn't understand Lightfoot's felonious side.

I'd stolen before.

In my teenage years, my father was detained by the government. His bank accounts were frozen and they seized his cars and property. This was a political thing after a military coup, and roving mobs were burning people like my dad alive, sometimes tethered to their families, thus creating a bonfire. My father was of the rare breed who attended to both broad strokes and details. He had a safe house and he made my siblings and I disappear to this barely completed house in the middle of nowhere. I'm not kidding. There was no bus route, and you had to hire a car to take you part of the way. You had to walk the rest. It wasn't a country stroll; it was a forced march. The road was unpaved, there were no street lights, and while it seemed safe, it looked scary as hell, and by 'looked' I mean it was darkness and crickets and flowing water. I did that trip alone a few times and I always expected some bandit to spring out at me. Nobody ever did, and I never heard of anyone getting robbed on the way there.

Deep down this way, a few folks, my father included, had built houses, expecting civilisation to grow from the end of the road. Except it never did, although this might have been part of the plan my father depended on. The result was our safe house, surrounded by a few empty dwellings, with no connection to the national grid, no amenities, no shops. It was better than burning to death.

My older brother and I had to cut the grass with machetes every other day, all to the cooing of wood pigeons and doves. I don't know birds; I know blisters from machete handles. The first time we did it, the grass was taller than me and it took a week to clear.

We did have a generator, but it presented a dilemma. When we turned it on it could be heard for miles around and the electric lights turned into a beacon. This was a problem since our task was to lie low. There was the matter of diesel. What would we do if it ran out?

But that wasn't our most pressing supply problem. We had no food, just some canned stuff that would disappear in days.

My brother Sam and I went exploring during the day. I didn't know the plan and thought he was just staving off boredom. He wasn't. He was casing farms. He didn't write anything down or scribble a map, or even indicate that he had noticed anything, but come nightfall he and I would steal out into the dark, navigating by whatever gods guide thieves.

We dug up yams, yanked maize off the stalks, stunned and abducted chickens and turkeys. I advise avoiding geese as targets for an agrarian crime spree. They are vicious and noisy.

We would take our ill-gotten gains and cook them for our younger sisters and brothers. At times we had to travel miles before we found a farm that didn't have dogs or a fence. We'd have to eat on the way. I was kind of low-key ashamed that neither of us knew how to make fire and had to use matches. On these occasions we would dig a hole, stuff it with grass and drop a yam in it, then set the pit alight. The fire stayed below ground level, so it wouldn't be seen from a distance, and the smoke was invisible at night. We would eat the yams by dipping them in palm oil, sometimes salt. We'd then drag the rest home on full bellies.

We didn't always succeed, and we starved sporadically. We would make do by chewing kundi, dried jerky-like meat, panla, and beef hide, undigestible, but hunger-killing.

Eighteen months of this we endured, and the surrounding farmers had to put up with thieves in the night. I wonder how much they knew, and how much they suspected. Sometimes our neighbours would bring us food. They knew there were kids in the house and never saw any adults, I guess. We ran the genny from eight to midnight on most days. Towards the end, Sam got into a torrid sex thing with a farmer's wife where she fell in love and started bringing us cooked meals.

While I couldn't recommend starving to anyone, that whole experience left me unafraid of shit like losing my job, not having any supplies, losing money, or any kind of deprivation. Once you've lived a life of not knowing where your next meal is coming from your outlook on life and luxury changes.

I told this entire story to Lightfoot in bits, over time, in my study and in the bathroom and while driving.

'Aren't you supposed to be blind? How can you be staring at me like this?'

Nothing from her. While Henrietta would laugh occasionally, Lightfoot never spoke.

6

Regardless of the first haunting with Henrietta or the second haunting with Lightfoot, the rest of my life was expected to go on. Including an expectation to be a husband, which I was fucking up; a father, in which I was lagging behind; a doctor, which I was barely managing; and a writer, which was poisoning my mind.

'What's going on with you?' asked Elise. 'You're not here. You're not with me. You tell me I'm distracted by my phone, but you're the one off with the fairies or the Jabberwocky or something.'

'You mean the Jabberwock. Jabberwocky is the poem.' It slipped out before I could control myself.

'Shut up, Tade. You're missing the point here.'

'Sorry.'

'Why is there blood on the towels?'

'What blood?'

'You think I don't look at the laundry? There's blood on your underwear, housecoat and towels from time to time.'

Yeah. Abrasions on the skin of the penis after too much rubbing.

'I have piles. You know that.'

'This isn't haemorrhoids. I am not stupid.'

No, she was not, but that didn't mean I was going to tell her the truth.

'Any other man and I'd think you were being unfaithful,' said Elise.

This was true. I didn't cheat, although not for moral reasons. I had a deep-seated belief in some form of Karma. So remember when I said there was no hell in Yoruba cosmology? Well, there may not be eternal punishment, but there are temporal consequences to offending. Eshu, the god of chaos, is allowed to make life on Earth difficult for you if you step outside your destiny. I know, it's weird, but I figured if I was a good person and didn't cause pain to anyone else, I would be fine too.

'I have some scratches. Down there,' I said.

'Show me.'

I glanced at Lightfoot, who was as bland as before and had seen me naked already, but this seemed different. I showed Elise.

'Jesus, what the hell, Tade?'

I could understand her consternation. It was discoloured, crusting in some parts, scabbed in others, raw and weeping in some. It looked worse than it was. Okay, it didn't, but all of this carnage healed pretty fast in my experience. And I was becoming quite experienced.

What happened next wasn't surprising, but I didn't expect it. A slight breeze and the smell of rotten meat, maybe a dash of Henrietta, but I'll be honest, I didn't see her this one time. I got erect. Couldn't be helped.

Elise looked at me with a disgust that matched my own. She slammed the door on her way out. That's when Henrietta appeared.

Since you're already up...

Back to my family doctor, this time with Elise in tow. No, I was in tow. Elise dragged me there.

'Your blood results are fine,' said the GP. She wore a bright red bindi that moved when her expression changed. If you're Hindu, that dot is symbolic of Bindu, which is where creation began, which can be reconciled with physics if you have time and three beers. I stared at the bindi rather than her eyes, and I didn't think she could tell the difference. 'You have a mild leucocytosis, but I'm not worried about that because of your... scratches down below.'

Another moment I will never live down. Showing a distinguished Asian doctor my junk and explaining the appearance.

'It's not infected?' asked Elise.

'No. Just abrasions of various ages, that's all.'

'What's wrong with him?' Elise had lost the rage and was now in concerned-wife mode. It was touching, I supposed, but I just wanted to get out of there before I died of shame poisoning.

'Compulsive masturbation,' she said. She didn't look up but continued to type. 'I'm giving you fluoxetine.'

'And that will stop it?' asked Elise, looking from me to the GP.

'It might.'

She was right. You could give fluoxetine for compulsive behaviour to good effect, as they say, but as I looked at Lightfoot and the flashes of Henrietta when I blinked, I wasn't optimistic.

I still needed a story to give to Francis Bacon's people. They didn't want the outline just yet, but they did need an idea of where I was going with the book and I didn't have a fucking clue.

My imagination flowered for every other project and even brought forth new ideas for short stories, books, screenplays, comics and console games. I even had an idea for a short musical about life on Mars. Just nothing for Bacon.

Whenever I started working on anything else Lightfoot made me feel guilty because obviously she was a hundred per cent for Francis and any deviation was slacking off. She stood there judging me like a schoolteacher. I found myself telling her my excuses, like how I had deadlines or needed variety to stimulate my imagination.

The worst thing is when I started the fluoxetine I felt restless, which happens as the serotonin rises, usually during the first week. I had a sense of internal motion, constant, and a need to do things, touch surfaces, bite into objects, throw rocks, stare, crash my car, and, yes, suicidal impulses. I felt like jumping from the roof of the hospital a number of times. I didn't want to, but I got a strong urge to. I wondered what it would be like to leap into space and fly for a while. Would I hear the sound of the ground hitting me? Would I feel my brain disintegrate? Would I lose consciousness or would I be aware of the pain until my heart stopped? I didn't want to die, but I sure spent a lot of time ruminating on it in that first week.

My guts went haywire too. I lost fluid from both ends and when I wasn't puking or shitting, I was groaning from the pain as my belly went into spasm. I would have stopped, but I already knew that fluoxetine could do this in the beginning, so I rode it out.

And the dreams. Oh, boy.

If you ever go on an antidepressant, don't load your subconscious with the paintings of Francis Bacon.

I woke up screaming every night for a month or so. Trap, who, night terrors aside, sleeps like the Qin Shi Huang's Terracotta Army, had to stay in bed with Elise while I took the couch. Such was the nature of my shouting.

With all those side effects in play, and adjustments of living arrangements, did the compulsive masturbation disappear?

No, it did not.

7

Once, when she didn't think I was in earshot, my mother described me at birth to a friend.

'A soothing, less-healthy-than-average baby. A slime mould of the womb.'

Yeah, I was soothing all right. Mostly because I wouldn't cry. I would wake up in the middle of the night, my eyes would be open, my nappy wet and my stomach empty. That's what my auntie said to me, anyway.

I was wheezy with bronchiolitis early on, and later, possibly asthma. I wasn't sporty as a child, but would take to physical activity as an adolescent.

Everybody knows growing old means becoming a puddle. You drip into this sludge, one muscle at a time. Your face droops like Indiana Jones's Nazis. When did I become a puddle? I used to be a shoot with fibrous branches for arms. Now I'm a slow-motion capture of a man becoming liquid, flowing by the grace of gravity to the floor, melting like the Wicked Witch, belly and tits first. My face used to be tautly applied to the bone beneath, but now? It is sliding away from my skull. Nothing dramatic, though. It's on the sly. One millimetre a year.

But this all came up because I had started to feel something different. I could feel parts of me dripping into something fleshy just outside my awareness. It was adjacent to reality, unfair in the way it cheated the senses. I could feel its efforts. I could feel its effects.

Have you ever had a dream so vivid you end up with memories of it for years afterwards? Decades pass and you wonder if it actually happened. Have you ever been to a place where you can hear the heartbeat of the world? There's this thing called The Hum, a low, droning sound that very few people hear in a few places in the world. The Taos Hum. The poet in me wonders if it's the engine behind reality, the unseen moving parts that keep things going. It's probably tinnitus, but...

I used to be someone people liked, or at least someone people could like. Now I was just another old puddle hamstrung by age and domesticity. What the fuck did a guy like me have in common with Francis Bacon who was free to live as he pleased, drink as he pleased, gamble as he pleased, take a beating as he pleased?

I should ground this chapter in something, an actual occurrence, otherwise it becomes me waffling on about imponderables, but literary structure can suck my dick.

Fine.

While looking for a story line for the novella I stared at a man dragging a bag behind him from Stoke Newington bus station like a reverse Khepri, that self-created dung beetle god. I contemplated a tyre track that had solidified in dried mud. I saw my dusty books as a metaphor for old and obsolete methods of thinking.

None of this means anything. It is all about what it seems to be about. You might be trying to draw thematic meaning, and you are a well-trained reader who has been taught to do that, but you are in the zone of my subconscious now. This is free association, and any thematic coherence is purely accidental. Or is it?

I only ejaculated twice while writing this part.

The problem with the whole undertaking was my rationality. It never let me go enough to enter that state of mind that allowed the irrational. Losing it might have led me to the promised land that I sought, but my thinking self was too adherent. I was well defended, remember. This was William Blake's 'Urizen', an obstacle to artistic expression.

Drugs, then. Entheogens. Chemistry at all costs!

Decades ago I smoked weed with a girl I liked. She was tall. Asian girl with typically long, glossy hair and beautiful brown skin. She didn't like me that way, though. She did like me in some way and she hung out with me. She had never smoked cannabis and wanted to. I had some. Next to her, I was Freeway Rick or something. I wasn't plugged in and I didn't have a supplier. I couldn't roll a joint if you put an Uzi to my head. No, I had weed because an ex-girlfriend of mine left some at my place. *She* had a guy who she would call and fifteen minutes later some kid on a bicycle would drop it off on the corner. But I didn't tell my guest any of that.

I mixed the cannabis with tobacco, also my ex-girlfriend's. Smoking had never been my thing.

Puff, puff, pass; puff, puff, pass.

On her, a spinning sensation. She went to my bed and fell asleep. Which was a damn shame because I had planned to attempt to kiss her. Couldn't do that when she was asleep. Oh, the humanity! I had willpower back then, even when operating in a purple haze.

It took trust for her to just drop off in my place and I wanted to capture the moment, so I sketched her. It captured her low-riding jeans, the curve of her belly and the dome of one of her breasts in her low-cut blouse. And that hair, of course.

When the weed kicked in, my thoughts started racing, and I wrote a sprawling interpretation of 'The Boy Who Cried Wolf'.

Puff, puff, pass.

You have heard this story before.

There is a small village, and in this village there is a shepherd boy and one day this shepherd boy is alone at night, watching his flock, when he sees a lone wolf approach. So he cries, 'Wolf! Wolf!' after which the villagers come running with machetes and cutlasses and pitchforks only to find there is no wolf.

As you know he does this three times and the third time the wolf persists, but the villagers do not respond. The wolf attacks and kills the sheep and the boy weeps, not, as most would have you believe, because he is ashamed of having tricked the other villagers, for he did not, but because he has lost his livelihood.

Without the means of making a living the boy goes into the village to beg for money. He hopes to build a new flock from scratch. What transpires is he sees things around each person. As they drop money in his bowl he perceives spirits, hobgoblins, ghosts, familiars, and, from time to time, Death itself. Though frightened, he learns to take chances and tell people what he sees. They do not always respond with gratitude, but, however humble, they always provide remuneration. In this manner his reputation grows and he begins to tell fortunes. One day, while looking at his own reflection in a brook, he sees the whole wolf episode again. The first few times he cried wolf were premonitions, but it looked so real that he was frightened. He remembers the smell of wet pelt on the phantom wolf, the drip of saliva from snout.

He lives for many years as an oracle in the village, one with unparalleled accuracy. He marries the butcher's daughter, a busty, corpulent girl who smells of the earth and whose heart is full of wonderful delicacies that he often intuits. Sometimes when they lie together his gift spreads out its tendrils and he dreams of the beautiful contrivances of her soul. In such a state he is able to see time itself stretch out in a grand curve, an arc over the sphere of space.

Given enough time, space and unlimited energy, that which curves will return to its origin. The oracle, who always thinks of himself as a shepherd, sees his own end.

In his fortieth winter the priest of a new god comes to the village. This god is malignant, spreading metastatic claws, driving other fetishes and idols out, insisting on adoption of its tortured man-child. The priest, who insists on being called a father, declares the former shepherd a witch and commands his followers to execute him. The auto-da-fé is calm, and the oracle serene as he burns to death. His wife, who knows this day has been foretold, observes the proceedings with veiled rage. People point her out in the observing crowd. She is never seen again afterwards.

After this, as is the custom, the priest rewrites the account, and the story of the shepherd boy turns into a cautionary tale for pranksters and his great life as an oracle is lost into eternity.

Puff, puff, pass.

I got hungry and I ate pasta al dente, not because I was a fancy-pants epicurean, but because I had no patience.

I covered my guest with a blanket.

She left the next morning, good girl tourist to the sordid land of hard drugs.

I failed in my attempt to make this a dream-logic exploration. My mind still tried to impose order, logic, pattern, system.

But I am telling you, this means nothing.

8

Being human, I adapted.

I left home with two sets of spare underwear and a lot of moist wipes. I took my rucksack everywhere. The original purpose of this was to heft books. I was, for my sins, a reader and my worst nightmare was to become stranded somewhere without a book to read. Like many bookworms, I couldn't tell you which book I would need, so I'd take more than one. E-book readers sorted out that problem for a while, but they fell out of my favour when research showed people retain less information when a thing is read digitally. Besides, I like the smell of print, and to stare at good cover art. I like how books fall open to frequently read passages. Judge me if you like.

Instead of reading material, I had sanitiser and small plastic bags so that I could take my rubbish home with me. The last thing anybody wanted was wads of semen-laden tissue in domestic waste baskets. That shit is biohazardous, or should be labelled so.

After weeks of use, the fluoxetine took the frantic edge off my compulsions, but I worked with people, and regardless of what you may have been told, people aren't stupid. Our speech is neutered at work because of policies and guidelines and culture and suchlike, but even if the flow of truth is like swimming through molasses, it does at least swim. So it was that concerns about me sluggishly made their way through the corporate structure to the people who were tasked with holding doctors to account. It moved by memos and corridor conversations and gossip and half-truths and meaningless, meaningful meetings.

In time, they summoned me.

It doesn't matter who 'they' were. What matters is that I answered to them and had to go when they called.

These things happen in a series of meetings. The first is a 'friendly' chat, an informal formal meeting. It's called informal, but it's minuted and filed away somewhere. This is Orwellian shit, where a thing doesn't mean a thing, where words are divorced from referents. You know what I'm talking about. You also see it daily.

I arrived at work and the department PA gave me an internal letter. I knew it was a problem because by then everything good came by email, everything bad in hard copy.

The meeting was by-the-numbers. We sat around a circular table, King Arthur style, innit? Nobody at the head of the table, eliminating hierarchical gradient from the meeting, which is bullshit. As I mentioned above, I am human, and we tend to know who the big primate is. This is just some nonsense corporate psychologists came up with to make themselves feel better about disempowering workers. The weaker workers are, the more elaborate these meaningless concessions to cosmetically flattened hierarchy are.

Jessie Lightfoot stood in the corner behind one of the bosses.

I made them wait as if I was answering an important text, but in fact I was placing a bet on my poker app. I resolved to put a betting limit on later.

'Thank you for coming in,' one of them said, on cue.

'Why am I here? I have work to do,' I said. That led to a small frown. It wasn't on the script. I was supposed to nod politely and wait for their questions.

'How's work?'

'Again,' I said, 'can we get to the point? Don't buy me dinner. Let's get to the checking if we have prophylactics.'

Frowns on both faces now. A part of me envisaged a cliff and me dancing on the edge of some cataract. But fuck them. I wasn't going to make it easy for them, no matter what. Blow, you cataracts and hurricanoes! Fuck you, managers, with your thought-executing patois and your sulphurous guidelines! Not quite what the Bard would say, but then again, he never had to deal with HR at the Globe.

'We've had some concerning reports about you,' one of them finally said.

'Unreliable, arriving late, leaving ward rounds without warning,' said the other, almost visibly hostile.

'I compliment you on allowing your amiability to slip,' I said.

'At least two staff members report seeing you in a state of... erm...'

'...Tumescence,' said the other.

'It was apparently very distressing.'

I knew what they were talking about. It had happened a week prior. The men's room had been occupied, so I went into the day room waiting for whoever was in there to get out. I turned to the wall when the women came in, but obviously not fast enough. None of that meant I had to play this game, though.

'I see. So, they were staring at my crotch?' I asked.

'What?'

'If there was tumescence, they must have been staring at my crotch.'

'I don't—'

'Did they take a photograph?'

'No, but—'

'Did they write statements to this effect? Signed and notarised?'

'We're just having a friendly chat.'

'So, you have the word of two staff members that I had… tumescence. You don't have photos or statements. You don't know if both of them colluded to get me in some kind of trouble.'

'I—'

'And they stared at my crotch. I find that offensive,' I said. 'I'd like to complain about this. In writing.'

'Well, hang on—'

'Exactly how tumescent was I supposed to have been? Did I have a semi or was it full-glory morning wood? I'd like to get it right when I tell my representative.'

I should have stopped there. The Bard should have whispered to me about protesting too much. I probably wouldn't have listened, but it would have been worth a try. But I worked myself up, got the old adrenalin going and the heartbeat pumping.

One of them coughed meaningfully.

I looked down.

My trousers were tented.

Damn.

And it was all going so well, too.

I drove home way under the speed limit.

Not a terrible outcome.

Two weeks of sick leave, although I wondered what meaning of 'sick' we were subscribing to. I had to disclose that I was being medicated for compulsions. They were understanding, but said I had to get the fuck out of there as one couldn't go around with a wooden willy searing all the delicate eyes of the nurses and support workers. Which is a load of crap. Let me tell you, hospital workers have seen it all. No person's junk bothers us.

The good news was I had free time to concentrate solely on Francis Bacon.

I looked in the rearview mirror, at Jessie Lightfoot. 'I'd offer you a high five, but I have to keep my hands on the steering wheel.'

I decided from the start I wasn't going to tell Elise about the sick leave. It would lead to too many questions that I wasn't prepared to answer. Like how far this thing had gone and for how long.

I didn't go home. I went to a café near the closest university to me and thought about Bacon. I needed to find another way to walk in his shoes. I knew I had to confront his masochism.

Why not now?

His father didn't know what to do with him. Daddy Bacon kept horses, trained them, even. He had some of the stable boys whip Francis. But Francis subsequently seduced them. His father then sent him to live with a friend who he thought would be a stabilising influence. Wholesome. Yeah, that didn't happen. What did happen is the guy started having sex with Francis and fell in love with him. Francis, for what it's worth, was sexually attracted to his own father.

I didn't know horses, I didn't know stable boys and, as far as I could tell, had no sexual urges towards my father. I had been whipped before, by my father, with a koboko, which is a piece of twisted leather that Yoruba people use on goats and children and rioting students. It hurts and leaves a welt.

I'd never solicited a beating, though. My reading told me Francis would wake up and paint each morning, then, early evening, he'd go gamble. Then he'd get himself good and beaten, buggered before or after. We're talking real lashings and punches here. He often turned up sporting black eyes and bruises. Peter Lacy, his first real love, almost killed him one time when he fell or was thrown through a plate glass window. This dude wasn't fucking around.

I didn't know if I wanted to go to find the whole BDSM scene.

I didn't know if that was a step I was willing to explore. I had brushed against it before. Twice.

Once, a girlfriend had asked if I was open-minded.

'In what way do you mean?' I asked.

She pointed under her mattress.

She had handcuffs, chains and manacles. She had something that looked suspiciously like a bear trap.

'I'd like to restrain you and inflict some mild correction,' she said. 'Mild.'

'What is "correction"?' I asked.

'Mild aversive stimulation,' she said. 'And I won't break skin.'

I did not want restraint and correction. I was a lot younger, and quite satisfied with vanilla sex, thank you very much. Which I had one last time and ran the fuck out of there. I had always been a live-and-let-live kind of guy, but I didn't like being tied up and I certainly didn't enjoy pain. I also wondered what kind of fantasy the woman harboured. A black African man chained up and being whipped by a white woman had connotations beyond sex. To me, at least. To me at that time. And she couldn't have been blind to that.

But how could I know how I would respond now? Most importantly, how could I understand Bacon's love of receiving violence without receiving violence myself?

Answer: I couldn't.

I had to find someone who would beat me up.

This wasn't as easy as it sounds. There's an anecdote about the filming of *Marathon Man*. There was a scene where Dustin Hoffman had to appear to be exhausted. Being a method actor, Dustin ran around the studio a few times and arrived breathless. Laurence Olivier, who was acting opposite him, asked him what he was running for and Dustin told him.

'Next time try acting,' Olivier is reported to have said.

'Next time try writing,' my friends would say to me if I told them I went to find someone to flog me. In truth, they would have thought I was a pervert, using writing as an excuse to indulge in my "unnatural wants". If I put out a query on Facebook or Twitter my mother would hear about it in two hours.

Classifieds, then? The café had half a dozen papers delivered every day. I checked the ads.

This is how I came to meet Danni, the Destroyer.

*

The Destroyer was a professional, by which I mean I paid her. I don't know if that makes her a sex worker or not. I have nothing against sex work, but people are trafficked, so I asked the Destroyer what her situation was. She laughed at me and asked me to sit in the corner facing the wall for an hour. She went out while I sat there.

I didn't find it sexy at all. To be honest, I imagined she was going to pull out two machetes and hack me to death while I was too handcuffed to mount a reasonable defence. I am pleased to report she did not kill me.

It was a bit of a scam, though, because most of the time the discipline was something I inflicted on myself while waiting on her hand and foot. And I wasn't alone. There were one or two other men, no women, who would be slaves to her. Most of the time there was no overlap, but sometimes she would chain me to the wall in her basement while the others were there (which she called a dungeon, but let's be real).

The whipping was both tame and lame. She had a cat o' nine tails that couldn't hurt no matter how hard you swung. I tried it one day when she wanted me to flog a different slave.

Danni the Destroyer was a big woman, easily six-three, six-four. Broad. A bit fat. Superb skin and supremely confident.

I saw her twice a week and after a month I told her I wasn't satisfied.

'I think I need to feel actual pain. This enactment isn't helping me get into the mind of a masochist,' I said.

'Because you aren't one.'

'Does that mean I'm Dom? Should I be paying to whip someone instead?'

She laughed at me and sent me to the corner. For free, which was kind of her, if you think about it. I was nervous, though, because Elise would soon be returning from work. It was essential that I was home before her.

'This isn't a binary state, Tade. Being either Dom or sub isn't a switch.'

'What am I, then?'

'A tourist. This isn't for you.'

I thought about that one. 'I'm not a tourist. I'm an anthropologist.'

A part of her heard me, though, because the next appointment things changed.

'I want you to change your posture. You're standing too erect, projecting too much confidence. I want you to slouch slightly, but not too much. Do it.'

I approximated what I thought she wanted.

'Don't make eye contact with me.'

I looked away.

'I didn't say don't look at me. Avert your gaze from my eyes.'

I looked at her from the neck down.

'Are you looking at my tits?'

'Yes.'

'Don't.'

I aimed my eyes at the demilitarised zone between her chin and her upper chest. This was a lot harder than it sounds. It didn't work the way Nicholson Baker books make this kind of thing seem.

'Go and buy me some mango yoghurt,' she said.

I did. She hurled it at the wall.

'I said *plain* yoghurt.'

'Er...'

'What did I say?'

'Plain yoghurt.'

I went and got plain yoghurt. Two pots.

'Oh, good. You'd have had to go back to get a second one.'

The Destroyer opened one pot and poured the contents over my head.

'I want you to lick it all off yourself. Quickly. I'm busy today.'

Somewhat challenging, but not impossible. I set to.

'Your back's getting erect again.'

I snuck a look at Lightfoot, who was still expressionless. Henrietta never appeared when I was with the Destroyer. I couldn't figure out why.

I licked the yoghurt off my left arm first starting from the shoulder, over my shirt, a bit bitter at the armpit from deodorant, the pit of my elbow, my forearm, my wrist, my palm, the back of my hand, the tips of the fingers, then the back of the hand, the palm, the wrist and on to the shoulder.

Contortions now, as I licked the tiny part of my chest that I found accessible. Breathing heavy now. I went foetal so I could get to my legs, but I was a chunky, five-seven guy, not a yoga instructor. I was muscular and I had generous belly fat. This was always a losing game.

'Take off your clothes, wipe your body off, and lick.'

I did this.

I knelt in front of my clothes, a middle-aged puddle man with a puddle of yoghurt-soaked fabric. She reached into the pile and pulled out my belt.

She doubled it, shook her head, then pinched the end tip. She wrapped the strap around her palm, leaving the buckle and about a foot of free leather to dangle.

'Turn.'

I did, backing her.

I heard in my mind Sam and Dave singing 'Hold on I'm Comin''. I remember that distinctly because it puzzled me. I hadn't listened to it since 2003 when I bought their greatest hits CD from Virgin Megastore on Oxford Street.

When you're flogged with a belt you don't feel the strap for the buckle. I knew immediately that she'd broken my skin. The pain was searing to start with, and with subsequent stripes I felt alternating throbbing and heat.

Yeah, I cried out.

Yeah, I hated it.

What the fuck, man, how do people enjoy this? It fucking hurts.

And I was paying for this.

Worst thing was I couldn't listen to Sam and Dave after this. Still can't.

I have suffered for my art. Tell everybody.

The Destroyer was surprisingly tender afterwards. I lay across her lap as she treated my back. Good, gentle hands. She put strips over some of the cuts and stitched one because as fate would have it, she was a nurse. Or used to be before she got a higher calling.

'So, anthropologist. What do you think?' she asked.

'Is it supposed to hurt?'

'You have nerve endings. Yes, it's supposed to hurt.'

'Then what's the point?'

'Excuse me?'

'Why do people... get hurt? This is just pain. It's not arousing at all.'

She didn't speak, but her hand snaked down my front and squeezed my limp penis.

'Are you here because of someone else?' the Destroyer asked.

'Yes.'

'This person enjoys pain?'

'Yes.'

'Do you know if it was sexual?'

'What do you mean?'

'Masochism isn't always sexual.'

Hmm. I had no idea if Francis Bacon got sexual gratification from his beatings.

The Destroyer warmed to her topic. 'Freud said a masochist is just a sadist with guilt. Guilt at the idea of hurting or humiliating someone is too high a price to pay, so instead the masochist identifies with and becomes the object of pain and humiliation. No guilt. Everybody wins.'

I knew this already. I also knew that, as usual, Freud's ideas on the matter were not universally accepted, nor did they have irrefutable proof. Some weeks earlier, I had tried to find Bacon in my psychotherapy and psychiatry textbooks and journals. I was surprised that the Destroyer knew so much, though. Perhaps I had underestimated her.

Her hand pumped up and down now.

'I'm more of a Behaviourist Theory fan,' she said. 'You couple the non-sexual object, in this case pain, with repeated pleasurable sexual action.'

She... coupled.

The Destroyer was wrong about the behaviourists, though. Or at least, she wasn't right enough. You can condition a response, sure, but to create a pathological masochist you also need problems with self-esteem and relationship-forming problems. Most masochists are not pathological.

I would have been predisposed to be a pathological sado-masochist because I had self-esteem issues and difficulties forming and maintaining relationships. We'll come to why later.

But all of this was academic, even as I seemed to watch from a distance as Destroyer put a salve on my welts and wanked me over her knee. I wasn't the masochist. Bacon was.

Reality wasn't that easy to understand. I was the one with the torn back.

The guy bent over the Destroyer's lap ejaculated violently and thrashed about like he was experiencing a seizure. His eyes rolled up like he was off on an out-of-body experience and his mouth opened showing all his teeth and a lolling tongue. A line of spit dropped to the floor.

Was he dead?

Hold on.

I'm coming.

9

Something happened to me, a thing related to being in pain most of the time.

The best way I can put it is, the rest of my life fell away, not all at once, but slowly, not enough to see day by day, but a pattern discernible after a month. Healing lashes are the worst, probably because delicate nerve endings and blood vessels are growing back. In that state any small movement can disrupt them or set them off. This is why it's best to rest and be still when you have healing wounds. But I couldn't admit to being wounded, and I had no official reason for bed rest.

Moving as slowly as possible became important. Avoiding jostling when in public, driving like a statue, and absolutely no running. I had to do all this hunched forward, slouched, because the Destroyer said I had to take this posture even between visits. My back muscles screamed out at this, but homo sapiens are so cool because we can get used to almost anything.

People around me started responding to my body language, even if they didn't know it. They started to challenge me more, and while I wasn't bullied, I was offered things that I would never have been offered had my posture been what it was before. Like the ECT rota.

Electro-Convulsive Therapy or ECT is one of the least understood and most effective treatments in psychiatry. Most people's opinions on this derive from *One Flew Over the Cuckoo's Nest*.

If I become mentally unwell, I'm having ECT. I've written it in my advance directive, though you can't make the treating team give you a treatment; you can only tell them what you don't want. You can suggest what you do want, though.

But none of the above is the point. The point is ECT is effectively administered by the anaesthetist who puts the recipient under and the specialist nurse who arranges it. Most areas have a supervising psychiatrist, however, and it is the most boring job you can imagine.

The last thing my mentor told me when I finished training was, 'When you get a job they're going to try to put you in charge of the ECT rota. They will dress this up like it's some kind of honour, and you, being such a new specialist, will think it's great to be offered. It isn't. Do not accept it.'

And I found this to be correct. The role is mostly administrative. Who does what and why. Filling out repetitive, boring and at times contradictory forms. And there are many forms. These forms are for safety in some ways, but in other ways they reflect dramatic fear of what the voting public do not understand, fear stoked by movies and TV shows. ECT is as safe as a tooth extraction, but you have to jump through dozens more hoops than dentists do to yank out your premolars.

I had already refused years earlier, so I was surprised when it came back to me. 'You know who should do the ECT rota? Tade.'

I resisted, but found it interesting that they would ask.

Normally, I would have mounted a robust verbal defence, but this time I just said, 'No.'

It stopped mattering. All things acquired a blurry margin instead of a sharp edge. Only the pain in my back was sharply defined. Destroyer wasn't a fan of painkillers, so I couldn't do pills. I was allowed analgesia if it stopped me from sleeping.

Elise had been talking for some time before I even registered her presence. That is how blurry life was.

'Sorry, what?' I asked.

'I said it's going to be an odd number since Jess broke up with Mark, but we can make it work.'

'Make what work?'

'The dinner.'

'What dinner?'

'What dinner? We've been talking about this for weeks.'

She had been talking for weeks. My mind was elsewhere.

'When is it?'

'Tonight.'

'Where?'

Elise's mouth dropped open. 'Here! We're the hosts, dummkopf!'

'Right, right. I knew that.'

I did not know that.

I also did not want strangers in my house. Well, not strangers. We had known these people for a minimum of ten years. No, I wasn't in the mood for visitors, but most importantly, it was my day to see the Destroyer. I didn't know if she would give me permission to miss the appointment. I didn't like to call her because she didn't like to be disturbed.

I jumped, because Lightfoot rushed towards me and stopped a few inches from me.

She screamed.

A kind of scream at any rate. Her mouth opened as wide as it could go and she seemed to be shouting, though no sound came out. She took breaths and yelled some more.

'Tade?' said Elise. Concern on her face. Heartbreaking. 'I'm calling the doctor.'

All I could think of was the dinner party was off. Inside, I was jubilant.

I should not have been.

The dinner was indeed cancelled, but our friends still turned up out of concern. I didn't talk to them, decided I was stressed, which is what the doctor said before she increased the dose of my fluoxetine. I stayed in the bedroom, lying on my side and listening to the muffled voices from the living room. Lightfoot kept moving back and forth, sometimes quiet, sometimes screaming. I had thought her a kind of harmless hallucination before then, but I started to wonder if she wasn't dangerous in some way. Could she harm me? Would she harm me? To shut her out I had to close my eyes, but with my eyelids down, Henrietta appeared and… the usual endpoint.

I found myself needing the edge that pain brought. I bit the inside of my cheek so hard I drew blood. But I felt better, less foggy, able to think in the moment. It gave me the courage to call the Destroyer.

She was not pleased. 'I was looking forward to this evening.'

'I'm sorry.'

'I do not want apologies. There will be correction. Loving correction.'

Later, Elise and I sat at the dining table, me eating the chicken soup she made for me, her pretending to eat a salad, but really just watching me. We had the opposite of the electricity you see between new lovers. We had mildew, rising damp, flaccidity.

Lightfoot darted forward suddenly, and I jumped, the chair making a sickening screech against the floor.

'What's wrong with you tonight? You're even jumpier than usual. I mean your new usual, of course,' said Elise.

'I'm… work is a bit difficult.' This was true. Work was challenging since I'd returned from sick leave, but that had nothing to do with my nerves. My thoughts were consumed with trying to get to Destroyer that night.

'You should take one of the pills,' said Elise. 'The ones you're supposed to take when you're feeling too anxious.'

I didn't like those. They made my thinking cloudy the next day. The irony of the clouds being present before the pills. Heh.

'I'm going for a walk,' I said.

I walked to the end of the street through pools of street light. Soon as I turned a corner, I summoned a taxi and I found myself at Destroyer's house within half an hour.

'I didn't ask you to come,' she said.

'No, but—'

'Be quiet. Let me think of what to do with you.'

I heard a voice in the background.

'Come up,' said Destroyer.

Inside, there were discarded clothes on the floor, not hers.

'Go to the kitchen, get me a glass of water, and bring it to the bedroom.'

I did.

In the room she was with a naked hirsute man with long blond hair and a beard that had seen more product than I had ever used in my entire life. She draped herself all over him. I took the water to her, but she indicated that it was for him.

'Thanks,' he said. 'So, what's your story?'

'Don't talk to the help,' said Destroyer. 'He's a doctor.'

'Truly? I didn't know you still did house calls,' he said.

'We never stopped,' I said. 'We call them domiciliary visits now.'

'Did I say you could talk?' asked Destroyer. 'Go to the corner. I'll call you if I need you.'

I watched blond guy plough into her and I heard her entreaties to him, encouraging him, begging him, forgiving him. Lightfoot watched me from the opposite end of the room.

Strictly speaking this was not in our contract.

Study for a portrait of the Destroyer.

She was thirty-one years old. She would say she was not from Manchester, by which she meant she was from a place called Hadfield.

'No, not Hatfield,' she corrected when this first came up.

Her father did something to do with tourism in the Peak District. She called him a lot and had long collusive conversations that I could not follow. Her mother did some admin work now, but before that managed five care homes. She suffered a massive stroke and it took a while for her to regain certain functions.

'Ten years of hard physiotherapy and speech therapy and coloured crystals got her back to secretarial duties. She's not who she was.'

Destroyer came to London to be an actor. She made some minor noise in Manchester doing theatre work and ran afoul of some local drug dealer.

'He wanted me to pay him in kind. I had money to pay in cash. We disagreed.'

London did not accept her as an actor. It was always close, always the next audition, always paying to attend this talk by that famous person. Bit parts and commercials and… shit, really.

'My closest brush with fame was when I heard Ridley Scott was looking for a Northern lass to play a Northern lass in a film. He was delayed by that volcanic ash thing that stopped flights and I was never invited back. Oh, and I saw Madonna once for about three seconds before a wall of bodyguard flesh blocked me from her.'

London did accept her as a manual worker.

With blond guy she was soft and gentle. He stared at me while she took him in her mouth.

Lots of actors do cleaning gigs and waiting gigs and eye-candy gigs. They also do parties. Standing around as the decorative flesh so that the successful can have an image that includes beauty and youth. Glittering lights, music. Some drugs, but not so much; Destroyer and her kin hoping the pixie dust of stardom would rub off on them.

It didn't. These events sucked out the little life force Destroyer had. There was nothing left in the tank for her to shine in her roles. Even less in the bank.

Hadfield was not an option.

She did some escort work to start with, to make rent.

'There was always more to spend your money on, more clothes, more acting classes, more travel to meet such and such director or to put you in a hotel lobby where one of the Hemsworths might just walk past.'

She couldn't tell me how old she was when she realised it wasn't going to happen for her. She did become depressed. She cried gallons, and when she ran out of tears she inflicted pain on others.

'It was already my preferred... activity. I just made others pay for it.'

She and blond guy finished. The room was thick with the smell of their exertions, the slime of human passing like a snail, as Bacon once said. But for the first time I had the beginnings of an idea of what to write. Portraits. Disturbing portraits that evoked the same feelings one got from Bacon's paintings. Distortions. Capturing human suffering. Or capturing my suffering. Disgust and horror.

Slime, slime, slime.

Destroyer made me stay long enough to be late enough to need an explanation for Elise. I had no marks to hide, and I had not had sex. But I was distracted with my project, and that was normal for me. Normal normal, not new normal.

I went home, shot straight up to my study, picked up a notebook and wrote for two hours straight without stopping. I got a cramp in my lower back and my neck from all the stooping Destroyer had me doing, but this was worth it. The first new pages of material since this assignment began.

I didn't read it over that night. I just basked in the glow of creation and deep down, in the place where I admitted hidden things, I was proud of myself.

10

I was so excited, I didn't touch the lunch that the Francis Bacon people were so generously paying for. I wasn't hungry, or maybe I just couldn't think about food at that time. I couldn't think about food at all. I was full of a manic energy that wouldn't go anywhere. Even when I slept my thoughts raced through options and dreams and not-quite fantasies.

I realised I was out of breath and stopped. They stared at me in silence. How long had I been talking? I reached for a glass of water. Sparkling, but it would have to do.

I talked about Lucian Freud and speculated about the rift between him and Bacon. Could they get me in with Freud's people? Could they? They had resources, didn't they? Could they? I drank more water as punctuation rather than to quench thirst. Could they? What did they think?

There were two of them, a woman and a man. Tarquin had been here, but only for introductions. He left for a meeting with some hot new talent. Those were his words and they drove spikes into me. I wasn't new, and I wasn't hot. Even when I was new I was old. Tade Thompson was never going to be on the 30-under-30 lists, or even 40-under-40. I was busy making one career and building my writing craft on the side. That doesn't make for a blazing, blistering debut novel complemented by my youthful good looks and the unending optimism of the young. My time was always going to be middle age; admission to medical school guaranteed that.

Wait. They were speaking.

'What?' I asked. I sprayed some water over the table because my mouth was full. I noticed that the woman ate nothing from that point onwards and I missed what the man said again.

'I'm sorry, you were saying?'

The man looked to the woman, then to me. 'I said we like it. You seem... excited about it and we hope that energy passes to the text.'

Hope?

'What do you mean?'

'I'm sorry?' asked the man.

'I asked what you meant.'

'That we like your proposal.'

'No, the other thing.'

'What other thing?'

'The thing with the energy. And the hoping.'

'...'

The man looked to the woman again, for help.

'Just that we're excited to see what you do with this, with the literary portraits.'

'Or do you hope to be excited? Which is it?' I had to restrain myself from brushing Lightfoot away. She kept bobbing in and out.

'I seem to have... that is, I don't know what I've said wrong, but perhaps we can start again.'

'We can start again,' I said. 'As soon as you tell me what you meant.'

'I—'

'Do you think I can't pull it off? That my ability is sub-par?'

Horrified smiles. 'Oh, no, no. We wouldn't be here if—'

'Then why do you hope?'

'Are you all right?' asked the woman. She had a wonderful mouth. In concern, it shrunk, and the lipstick made it seem like an improperly healed surgical wound. The kind that gets infected with *pseudomonas aeruginosa*. If it did, that perfect skin would bubble and distend, and when it cracked open the air would be full of ichor and the sweet smell of gas gangrene. Each time the muscles flexed gas would be forced out in a fart of putrefaction. I wanted to kiss the mouth, the wound.

I had missed what they were saying again. I needed to get back in the moment, in the now. Mindfulness. Breathe.

The man was on the phone and the woman was clearly leaning away from the table. The waiter floated towards us like a moth, but bounced off when she saw the curt head shake the woman gave him.

The ambient music had the bassline from that Iron Butterfly song, 'In-A-Gadda-Da-Vida', but not quite. It was only the bass, none of the keyboard. It bugged me that I couldn't figure it out, this bastard version of a song I loved.

People were talking at me, but I just wanted them to shut the fuck up so I could work out why this damn song wasn't what I expected it to be.

I looked up and I had an audience.

The hell was going on?

'You all right, mate?' Someone in uniform now.

'Why wouldn't I be all right?' I asked.

'D'you want to come with us to the ambulance?'

Ambulance? Wait, where were the Bacon people? We were in a meeting, weren't we?

Lightfoot followed us out of the restaurant. She was laughing for the first time.

Study for portrait of a psychiatrist as a psychiatric patient.

'They said you were rambling,' said Elise. 'You just sat there and didn't make any sense.'

The ambulance took me to the emergency department and while they didn't feel the need to admit me, they didn't feel comfortable sending me back into the wild, so I had to call someone to pick me up. Elise cut short her working day just to bring me home. She wasn't amused.

'I had a meeting,' I said. 'I was excited about the concept. It got out of hand, is all. I'm fine.'

'What meeting?'

'With Francis Bacon's people. We had a noon thing. I have to explain what I'm writing.'

'There wasn't any meeting, Tade.'

'Yes, there was. We had a reservation and everything.'

Elise shook her head. 'You turned up at this place, walked past the podium, and sat at a table that was being bussed. The place was in the weeds because it was lunch hour. The hostess tried to ask if you had a reservation but you kept waving her off. You were talking to yourself. You had no guests, Tade.'

'That's preposterous,' I said. I had never used that word in my life. I did yank out my phone to call Tarquin, my agent.

'Hey, Double-Tee!'

God, I hated how this man spoke. 'Tarquin, how did your meeting go?'

'What meeting?'

'You know, the hot new next-big-thing you were going to meet this morning?'

Nervous laugh. 'You know you're my only hot big thing, Tade!'

'No, seriously, when you left, you said—'

'Left where?'

'Lunch.'

'What lunch?'

I took a deep breath because my lungs wouldn't fill up. 'I'll call you later.'

Elise cocked her head. 'You need a holiday.'

'"Thief's Theme"! That's the song. Ugh, it was driving me crazy!'

Elise raised an eyebrow.

'It's a Nas song. The restaurant was playing an instrumental version.' I realised this probably sounded mad. 'It doesn't matter.'

'Shall we go home?'

I sat in a bath with water that cooled from hot to lukewarm in record time. When you've been to the emergency department or hospital there's a smell, industrial disinfectant or some shit, that you get maybe from the waiting room. It lingers on the body and in the mind. A bath is required.

My phone beeped with notifications. Poker. I called. I raised. I folded. Then I let the app use my playing pattern to decide what moves to make.

Lightfoot looked on.

'You could make yourself useful and scrub my back, you know,' I said.

The door swung open. 'Who are you talking to?' said Elise.

Study for portrait of writer's wife.

Elise is from Sierra Leone, or at least her parents are.

One day, when she was eleven, her mother arranged for her to visit their home country so that she could imbibe some culture. Ostensibly. At Heathrow, her older cousin Ruth saw her off and said she'd been on a similar trip a few years before, that it would be fun.

They landed at the airport and she was to join seven other girls of similar age, chaperoned by an older woman, in a village for some gentle enculturation.

They told tales, they sang songs, they slept on mats and mattresses, they learnt cooking. Maybe they got taught about boys and men, about penises and semen, about what to avoid, about illicit touching, about pregnancy.

But none of this was the true reason for the trip.

One evening the girls were joined by several older women, some of them quite robust.

'It's time for you to become women,' said the original chaperone. 'You must not speak of this, especially not to anyone younger than you.'

They split off into groups.

Elise went into one room with two women.

They told her to take off her underwear. She told me she felt some disquiet at this point, but they were aunties, and she trusted them, so she did. They gave her a wrapper to tie loosely around her waist. They asked her to lie down and spread her legs.

'No,' she said.

Every instinct in her told her to flee. Her spirit was already straining for the door, although her feet were rooted to the spot. The flickering of the kerosene lamp towards the air current seemed to match what her heart wanted.

The bigger woman grabbed both her arms from behind and flung her to the raffia mat. She sat down on Elise with her gigantic arse. Under the woman, flailing ineffectually, she became a pinned bug, trapped by physics and implacable tradition.

The other woman dragged a wooden stool between Elise's thrashing legs. She had something sharp that glinted, but Elise didn't know if it was a knife or a razor blade.

'Easy, girl. Easy. It'll be over soon.'

Elise could not breathe under Big Arse because her chest was compressed. She heard cries from far away and she realised that what was happening to her was happening to every girl in the group.

The woman's hand flashed forward like a scorpion's tail. Elise felt white heat in her crotch and a jolt of rocket fuel in her veins. She threw the fat woman off her, flashed out of the door and ran into the night, warmth streaming down her legs.

She fled into the bush, barefoot, bleeding, with only her top on. Behind her, shouts, screams, footfalls as people gave chase.

Fear and pain still powered her, and she scrambled up a palm tree, though till this day she cannot remember how she did it without breaking her neck in the middle of the fucking night. She held on to that tree trunk for dear life.

'I actually thought they meant to murder me,' she said.

Her memories are no doubt distorted, but she said she stayed up that tree for what seemed like an entire day. They found her and asked her to come down, but she didn't, calling for her father, yelling the whole time for him to come and save her.

The women discussed ways of getting her safely down.

Blood loss, hunger, tiredness, those things brought Elise down.

Weakened, she could no longer resist effectively. It was supposedly taboo for any male to be in the vicinity of the ceremony but they made an exception because they were scared Elise was going to fall and die. They got a ladder and a wiry youth monkeyed up and carried Elise down.

They took her straight back to the hut, spread her legs and cut her pudenda. They cut off the labia majora and some of the labia minora. They sliced away the clitoris. They sang joyful songs while they did it. Elise passed out and became delirious.

She was in hospital for twenty-one days. She got septicaemia and on day seven her blood stopped clotting. She had numerous packed cell transfusions and her entire blood volume had to be replaced. She got hepatitis. She had an HIV scare, but it was a false positive.

She got urinary retention because the urethra closed up, which contributed to kidney failure, although septicaemic shock didn't help.

She somehow survived all of this, but six months later, when her periods began, she had haematocolpos, blood stuck in her vagina, because her vaginal opening was too scarred and had healed over. She got a pelvic infection because why not and bacteria love static blood.

'I lost that entire year because it was too traumatic and I was delirious a lot of the time.'

But she survived.

Ruth turned up at their house for Elise's birthday the following year.

'I punched her in the fucking face and kicked her in the boobs,' said Elise. Her parents had to drag them apart.

'It happened to me too,' said Ruth, wiping blood from her nose.

'And because you kept quiet, it happened to me,' said Elise.

Fucking hell.

The life of an African girl.

When I met Elise she wouldn't let me go down on her. 'Because of the smell,' she would say.

'I don't mind,' I said. What? I didn't.

'I do.'

She wouldn't even let us fuck with the light on. We'd been together two years before I ever saw her fully naked, and even that was an accident of showering schedules.

Elise could only climax in specific circumstances. It took a lot of cajoling to find out why, and to hear the story.

'Want to come in here?' I asked. 'With me?'

She touched the water and withdrew her hand. 'Tade, this water is freezing. Get out of there, now.'

So it was. I hadn't noticed.

But I successfully avoided the topic of my hallucinatory lunch.

11

Standing up in my study, staring at photos of 7 Reece Mews, of the mess within. It wasn't a mess, though, was it? It was more of a focus for artistic play, where fragments of ideas could collide with each other and produce the kind of accidental meaning Bacon talked about. Sort of. Bacon couldn't be trusted on the matter of his intentions or process. There is what he said, and what he did, and what he wanted to be seen. Brand control, innit?

I wasn't a painter, so there was no point hoarding a bunch of images, but my equivalent was books. I remember that the first book I touched was *Energy and Civilization: A History* by Vaclav Smil. I stroked the spine. I loved books, not just the words or pictures within, but the objects themselves. I loved cover art, back copy, the copyright page, the acknowledgements, the backmatter. I loved that smell old yellowed books had, but not so much the faintly chemical smell of newer paper.

I threw the Smil down in the middle of my study.

I stared at it.

I bent, picked it up again.

I tore off the cover. Surprisingly I didn't feel any frisson of fear, which I would usually feel when I mistakenly damage a book. I tore the preface out, crumpled it and dropped it to the floor. I was learning new things with each page I ripped. God doesn't strike you down with thunder just because you damage a book.

Growing up, my mother wasn't a big one for books. Which is an understatement. She taught me how to read and how to write, but after that I was left to my own devices when it came to procuring books.

When I was done with the Smil, I cut *The Turn of the Screw* by James. It was a Norton edition too. I slashed lengthwise and the paper floated down, mixed with the Smil.

There were three books in my house when I was a kid. The Holy Bible, King James Version, which was my younger brother's baptismal bible; *Alice's Adventures in Wonderland* and *Through the Looking Glass* by Carroll, a hardcover left by tenants who lived there before us; *The Adventures of Tom Sawyer* by Twain, also hardcover, also left behind. These are books I read repeatedly because I had no others. My mother's main interest was pleasing my stepfather and my main interest was avoiding my stepfather's feet. We never went to bookshops or libraries. At that stage, I'm afraid to say, I was nervous of libraries and bookshops because I only knew them from TV, though attracted to them at the same time because of the books.

Roget's Thesaurus. The pages were like ribbons, like threadworms. There is a pleasure in destruction and I was getting drunk on it. I suspect I was laughing, but that might be a false memory. It feels like I should have been laughing because I am euphoric just writing this.

For two years, I didn't go to school. My mother moved us, my sister and me, from Wimbledon to Lagos without a proper plan. No arrangements were made for us to be educated. There was no arrangement for remedial lessons. My sister and I were stuck in a city where we didn't speak the language or understand the culture. With no books.

I wandered all over the place. My favourite spot was a burnt-out bus, where I would pretend to be the driver and conductor. I didn't understand the danger, and one day, rushing out because I heard my aunt call out for supper, I got slashed on sharp twisted metal, one gash on my shoulder and one on my knee. I bled freely and I have the scars to this day. In hindsight, I should have had stitches, and my aunt would have known that since she was an auxiliary nurse. But she didn't take me to hospital, which I think had to do with money, instead doused the wounds with hydrogen peroxide, which bubbled like lava when it came in contact with blood. Hello, new plaything. Didn't get a tetanus shot either. I suffered the wrath of my mother when she came back from whatever work she was doing at the time. No more fantasy bus driving for me.

My cousins looked down on us, of course. We were the poor ones. And they didn't know who my real father was, making me a *de facto* bastard. Back then, and today, as far as I know, if you didn't know your father or what village you came from, you were an object of scorn. I knew my biological father from a photograph. I had a vague memory of him in front of a fireplace talking to my sister and me, and one evening, talking to both of us through the front door. My mother locked us in to fuck off to a party somewhere. My dad stayed on the other side of the door, sat on the floor, playing word games. But these were fragmentary memories.

How to Write like Tolstoy by Cohen. Shredded, added to my brand-new literary compost heap. I had two papercuts on my index finger, which I stuck in my mouth.

It's not that there was no effort to get us into schools. The efforts were desultory and ineffective. We'd go to some local school, sit in class for a few days and be unable to return. I have no idea why. We didn't qualify in some way. Not academically, because I was inquisitive. Not behaviourally, because my stepfather had beaten the spirit out of me. I don't know. Nobody told us why. What I do know is that after two years, it was hard to adjust to a routine of daily attendance, so I used to bunk off and wander away or feign belly aches. I found it hard to pay attention.

My stepfather whipped both my sister and me as incentive to do better at school.

God, I hated that motherfucker till the day he died.

Roberto Bolaño, *2666*, took a long time to rip up, but by this time I was enjoying the act itself even more, so I didn't mind. I had a bottle of water. I opened it and emptied it on the pile of paper. I remembered some acrylic paints I had lying around. I emptied the tubes of paint all over the paper. Not quite 7 Reece Mews, but a good start.

I smeared paint on the attic door and the walls. I wiped it on my sleeve and my skin. I mixed brown by making orange from red and yellow, then adding blue progressively until I got the burnt umber I was looking for. I flung this at the skylight like diarrhoeal shit.

I typed for three hours straight, only stopping to masturbate twice when I tried to rest my eyes and saw Henrietta laughing. Papercuts don't go well with self-defilement.

I looked to Lightfoot for approval, but she was as blank as usual.

'Fuck you, then,' I said.

Bergen, *What the F*; *Saturnalia: An Anthology of Bizarre Erotica* edited by Scott. *Afrofuturism* by Womack. *Systems of Survival* by Jacobs. All went in the pile.

I looked around at my study, my pile of inspiration. I had more books to rip, but it would take a while. I considered running the pages through a shredder and adding that.

I felt something, but there was no specific word, no definitive descriptor for it. I expected something. Rather, I knew something was coming to me. Something familiar and adjacent to reality. I'd had this feeling before. Not a phantasm like Lightfoot or a succu-

bus like Henrietta.
   This would be more substantial.
   This would be more dangerous.

12

'I want to try something new,' said the Destroyer. 'Take off your clothes.'

I did as I was told.

'It's outside our contract, I'm afraid.'

'Will it hurt?' I asked.

'Most likely.'

'Will it leave a mark?'

'Not where anyone can see it. It presents more of a psychological mark. It's the crossing of a psychological barrier.'

'Why do I need to cross this particular barrier?'

'You'll see in a minute. Come over here.'

I did.

'Put your hands down my waistband.'

I did.

Oh.

My hands closed around a plastic phallus.

'You said the work you're trying to do is to channel an artist, right? And the artist was gay, you said? Well, you can't embody him by flirting with masochism. You need to bottom out, pun intended.'

'But I'm not gay.'

'You've never had homosexual experiences?'

Sure.

Boarding school. A guy two years my senior called Shining Black because he was so dark that his skin shone with a slightly blue-black iridescence. He was completely immoral and vicious. I woke one day with his hand on my crotch and his index finger across his lips. He wanked me till I came and warned me that if I ever spoke of it he would kill me. Literally kill, not metaphorically. Shining Black was so wicked that young me had no reason to doubt his word. He was a serial rapist, too big for me to fight, too sly for me to flee from.

Fifteen years later I remember a Radio 4 news bulletin that listed four black men who were being sought 'to assist the police in their enquiries'. Shining was one of them.

That doesn't count, though. What counts in this context is the time in my late twenties that I went to the gym with my friend and we showered together. It was the first and only time that I felt some twinge of desire at the sight of a male arse. I got over it, but it surprised me. I didn't think I was capable of those kind of feelings.

I didn't tell the Destroyer any of this. I didn't even want to include those events in this account and I experienced one of those slow-downs I told you about. Shame.

'No, I've never had homosexual experiences,' I said.

'All right. This isn't one either. You'll be with me, but still experience what your artist subject probably did. In a safe place, and you can stop me at any time.'

'I see.'

'Do you want to try?'

No.

'Yes.'

This really is the most difficult thing to write. This entire page has taken me a week. That's the kind of hesitation I'm dealing with.

She opened her jeans, asked me to kneel, and put the thing in my mouth. She did this for what seemed like forever. I could smell her, and this helped me get over my disgust, although I felt debased. I still do.

When she tired of this she made me turn around and drenched my hindquarters in K-Y. Cold as hell. She could have at least warmed it up.

She was slow, she was as gentle as you could expect, but it still hurt like hell.

'Tade, you have to relax. Breathe into it.'

'I am relaxing. It's hard to relax with this kind of pain. I am also breathing. Painful, still.'

'That's the pain of your repression,' she said. 'I expected better from you.'

She withdrew, annoyed, and she scourged me for so long that I used the Word for the first time.

I sat on cushions for a while after that, and not just because of the lashes. How do people do that for pleasure? What the fuck, Francis?

I retreated to my attic, to my nest, a place to lick my wounds, metaphorically.

I sat in the paper mess, then dropped supine. There was a moth on the ceiling, at an angle to the light. I remembered a long passage from an English textbook which consisted of two pre-teen boys arguing about whether something was a butterfly or a moth. Lepidoptera. Who gives a fuck? Flattened wings and nocturnal was probably a moth. Dull pattern, the colour of shit. Which was how I felt: dull and shitty.

I didn't feel like writing, which wasn't usually a thing for me. I didn't get blocked. I just sat down and let the nonsense pour out.

Some days, there would be nuggets. Not chicken, gold. Most days, it would be mediocre pap. The rest of the time, it would be bad. I didn't do inspiration or moods or the muse, or any of that lot.

I figured I would just rip up some more books and squirt some more paint. I saw the pile of Bacon books. I had read them; I had underlined, bookmarked, scribbled opinions, everything that I would ordinarily do when studying a subject.

I couldn't tell you what moved me, but I flipped through the photographs of 7 Reece Mews and tore out one page.

Stared at it.

Flicked my gaze to Lightfoot.

Stuffed the page into my mouth.

It takes fifteen minutes to properly masticate a glossy, high-quality sheet of paper into the kind of paste that you can swallow. I did this. Your eyes water when you try to eat paper.

I ripped another page.

And another.

I would absorb Francis Bacon one way or the other.

Morning light through the window. I had been eating the book all night. The inside of my mouth was red hot with cuts. My belly was distended and loud with borborygmus. When I stood up, I had to clutch my arse from pain and from the acute need to take a shit.

I made it down the ladder without killing myself and entered the loo.

It must have sounded like a war zone to anyone outside. Maybe too soon for Trap to wake up, but Elise definitely would have heard.

I passed lava and when I stole a look, wasn't surprised to see bright red blood.

I flushed three times.

It would have made a great Tony Orlando song: *Flush three times!* Not as romantic, though. Probably anti-romantic. Does anybody except me even remember Tony Orlando anymore?

I opened the windows, sprayed all the air freshener we had, and took a long shower. I attempted to brush my teeth, but forget it. Too many cuts.

I sloshed mouthwash in there and screamed with pain, but persisted.

I felt something cold on my left leg and I saw a line, a drop of bloody fluid snaking down my calf.

I cleaned myself again.

I looked at myself in the mirror. Curious. I couldn't see Lightfoot's reflection. That had never occurred to me.

'Are you a vampire?' I asked. 'I have some blood for you, if that's the case.'

I looked older. In fact, I looked my age. I had always been young-looking because of my round head and my cheeks. My face seemed angular now, my eyes sunken, my cheeks drawn. Like someone had stuck a needle into me and drained my élan vital.

'Why do you need to do any of this?' I asked myself.

Why?

It wasn't money. I had a bit of that, even though I wasn't rich. I had enough that I could do pretty much whatever I wanted. I could holiday anywhere I wanted, eat whatever food caught my fancy, buy any clothes I liked the look of. Besides, it's not like the advance would be life-changing or anything. No.

Fame? I wasn't a household name, but I was known enough. In fact, this Bacon book was going to be a problem because of the frankness of the studies. The yucky scatological vibe might evoke *Finnegans Wake*, but how many people read Joyce outside academia anymore? Notoriety. Infamy. This is what I'd be skirting with. No.

Did I want to be loved? Consciously, not particularly. I'd always taken the view that a few people loving you was best. Love is something I felt too intensely to scatter amongst the crowd. No.

Really, though? Most people want to be loved. Was I lying to myself?

Study for a portrait of the writer.

What is the origin of love? What is the root of it? How do you learn to love? Who teaches you love? How do you get conditioned for love?

For me, it always came back to my mother. Remember her?

The reason I didn't give a shit about the love of many was because I didn't have the love of my mother. Like I said before, she couldn't love me because of the rape, and right there is why my relationship with my mother was destined to be a little strained, to use British understatement.

I can't tell you if touching me made her skin crawl, but I can tell you she avoided it as much as possible. I can tell you that in childhood I only recall her hugging me one time, and it was when I was ten and she'd just returned from Hong Kong, a group hug with me, my sister and my brother. It occurs to me that my stepfather didn't meet her at the airport. This was a tumultuous time between them. He ramped up the beatings and had affairs. My younger brother was kidnapped, and returned home after three days like some kind of messiah. It sounds alarming, but this kind of thing was not unusual at the time. Even I escaped an attempt.

Two black-clad guys on a motorbike tried to take me. I don't know why films make this look like an efficient way to commit crimes. I was walking along on an errand and heard an engine rev behind me. I saw these hands grabbing for me. I ducked and spun around in the opposite direction. They turned, but this wasn't motocross. When they were almost on me I turned again and sprinted away down an alley. I hid in an alcove and waited for I don't know how long. Time is different when you're a child. I went home and the only one I told was my sister because by this time my stepfather and mother had gone fucking insane with breakup and makeup shenanigans. She kept shipping us to different homes, then going back to him. For about a year my sister, my mother and I lived out of one room.

It was the smallest space I have ever lived in, but, out from under the influence of my stepfather, I blossomed for a brief period. On some days my mother wouldn't or couldn't even look at me, which allowed me to spend as much time outside the single room as I liked. I made friends. I experimented with smoking cigarettes and passively inhaling ganja with my neighbour Lucas. I discovered pornography this time, not just a side-effect of buying comics from the same shop. I had no fucking clue about girls, but then, neither did any of the kids I hung out with. I walked all over the place, exploring, climbing trees, sneaking into a Coca-Cola plant and stealing water. Don't ask me why I stole water, because I don't remember. It might have been a dare. It might have been because I was thirsty from walking around so much. It might have been because the bottles, clear as the Invisible Man's shit and made of glass, were attractive to me in some way and I liked them. I stole two.

I got beaten up by a kid who couldn't hear or talk. He was larger than me and I suspect I had it coming, but I don't remember. I wasn't a great fighter, not at that time, but I had experience of taking beatings, and that gives you an edge in hand-to-hand combat.

I didn't know how to relate to people generally back then. I could get along with a certain type of older person. Readers, slightly anarchic folks, people who talked to me directly as an individual instead of shooting their usual canned speech at children. The people I spent most of my time with were at least ten years my senior. With kids my own age I would be silent. I'd go along with whatever they were doing but wouldn't say anything.

Do you know where your children are? My mother certainly didn't.

The problem is children react to this kind of neglect. I did. I got into a lot of fights from the age of eleven and only stopped when I turned seventeen. Between those ages, the Ages of Raging as I like to call them, I developed a shell. I became hyper-reliant on myself and decided that I didn't care if people liked me or not. It worked for a while, but it was a front of course. I wanted people to like me because I earned it, not because of who I was. Or I wanted the kind of respect that couldn't be taken away. The kind that academic achievement or winning martial arts contests bring.

I could give up this Bacon project and go back to writing fantastical stories of aliens and clones. I already had my validation. Prizes and cash.

I kept going. In point of fact, by this time I thought I would just finish but never submit it. This book would go in a vault and disappear. I would pay back the advance and that would be that.

And yet I kept chewing up paper and crumpling some for my psychic nest.

I kept getting bursts of creative output, and the book grew.

It was three weeks before Destroyer took my call again. She said she wasn't angry with me. She was, instead, delaying our next meeting for my own good.

'I wanted you to heal,' she said from behind me.

Her hands were on my shoulders and she maintained a steady rhythm of penetration. It was still painful, but not as much. Maybe because I chewed some codeine tablets before stepping into her flat.

Or maybe I was getting used to it.

I never came during these sessions. I took the humiliation.

I came home and I wrote for hours and hours.

When I took a break it was because my fingers ached. I cracked my neck, stretched, stood up.

Which is when I realised Lightfoot was gone.

13

At first, when you start to lose weight from some pathology, like, say, cancer, people tell you you're looking great.

That's what happened to me. I'd get into work and my colleagues would tell me whatever diet I was using was working, or ask me to share my workout tips. I was definitely leaner and my clothes were hanging looser on my frame. That was because I had a diet that consisted of cellulose sourced from paper. My tummy muscles felt lax and the curve of my spine was abnormal because the Destroyer made me slouch all the time.

At some point I deteriorated from fashionably lean to underweight and it showed. People transitioned into a kind of faux worry. They seemed concerned about my health, but in actuality they were concerned with their own. What's wrong with this guy and is it contagious? Can't he do the polite thing and take his sickness out of my face? Distancing strategies among primates. Other animals too. Bees will kick other bees out of the hive if infected with foulbrood, and the normally social lobster will avoid virus-infected ones.

My brain still worked, though. I may have looked ten years older, but all my neurons were firing as required.

Didn't matter. People told other people who told other people.

'You need to take sick leave,' said my direct boss in a new meeting, fortified by Human Resources.

'I'm not sick,' I said.

'I am a doctor. You are sick,' said my boss. 'Your muscle mass is less than it was six months ago, you're cachectic, your face is sallow, your eyes are bloodshot and, to be honest, you look like you have cancer.' AIDS went unspoken, but loud and clear.

'I don't have cancer.'

'How do you know? Have you had a blood test? Did you check tumour markers?'

'I've had a test.' Not tumour markers though. I should have done that.

'You are wasting. You have to find out why your muscle and adipose fat is melting away, Tade.'

Oh, *that*.

I knew where my flesh was disappearing to.

It was a sculpture.

Study for a portrait of the writer.

I have never been very tall, but I became muscular as soon as I got out of my gawky teenage years. Elise said I was made of circles. Bulging muscles, not large, but rounded and ever ready to punch. I trained first in karate, then taekwondo, then some mixed martial arts. I was good, not great.

Martial arts calmed me down. The time I stopped fighting when I was seventeen? That was why. Training exhausted me and sparring served as an efficient outlet for my rage at being unloved.

You do well in hand-to-hand combat if you don't fear pain and you train. I didn't fear a hit to the face. I worked out till my belly was hard and I could take hits there. And you'll recall that my stepfather had trained me to absorb kicks to any part of my anatomy.

I was at my best in university, of course, but that discipline followed me.

My hair started flaking off when I was twenty-one. I expected this because my father was bald from a similar age; I made peace with it, and things like Rogaine or a toupee were for lesser men. My gut grew ten years after that. That was genetics combined with diet, I guess. I liked food. I still worked out, but what I got for my pains was a big belly over hard muscle. I could live with that. I'd seen fat kung fu masters and my sparring was still effective. I used to be fast and strong; now I was experienced and strong. More brain than brawn to keep up with the youngers.

When that hardness started to abate, I wondered what was happening. That's where the sculpture came in.

About the time Lightfoot disappeared I started seeing a new object in my peripheral vision on the left side.

At first I didn't attend to it, thinking I was experiencing some kind of visual phenomenon, like a floater or something. Then I realised I only saw it when I was in my study and never when I closed my eyes. Henrietta still had dominion over my eyelids. It seemed like a drop of viscous fluid hanging in the air at first, translucent like K-Y gel, about the size of a rugby ball and the shape of an amoeba. Over time it became more and more opaque, and the colour changed to bright red. It seemed to grow as I lost weight. I started to think my belly fat was going there and nothing could convince me otherwise. Other than growth, it didn't move. It darkened to mauve.

'Jessie Lightfoot, where the fuck are you?' I asked the empty attic.

I experimented. Using just my willpower, I created a bulge in the side of the mass. Then I made it flatten into a disc. I got elaborate, pulling out horns and tentacles, twisting them into pretzel shapes, a mild distraction. I didn't think anything of it until it started pulsating.

If I concentrated in a quiet room, I could hear the beating of a heart. I put my hands on my own chest to see if it was the same. It wasn't. I had a tumour outside my body, fed by my own flesh, which I could, to an extent, shape. To an extent. It kept growing in size, and no matter how much I ate, I kept shrinking. At least I knew where the food was going.

My skylight sprung a leak one night and I came up to work one morning to find my keyboard drenched and my mouse borked. This shouldn't have been a problem since I mostly worked in longhand and transcribed. The problem was I still had to get all those ink scrawls into the computer and telepathic computing isn't a thing yet. I wasn't rich enough to have a personal assistant. I ordered a new keyboard, but the leak continued. I wrote to the sound of constant dripping water. It occurred to me, later, that it hadn't even been raining. Where was the water coming from? Was it even water? By this time I had a measuring jug to collect the liquid. I'd stop writing and empty it every hour or so. Now I was curious. I tasted the collected liquid and I was surprised and not surprised to find it salty. Like tears. Or sweat.

Where would that be coming from? The sea is miles away. Even if there was rain, it wouldn't be salty, although I remembered one instance of salty rain during a cyclone when I was in the South Pacific. I lived right next to the sea, as in I could take my lunch break in the Pacific and get back to work in minutes. I'm fairly sure what I tasted was sea spray, not rain, but salty rain sounds more sensational and it's a better story for dining out.

I looked left at the sculpture. My eyes hurt because I always had to keep them still, but shift my focus left, which was weird and migraine-inducing. The surface glistened, moist, and whatever fluid was on it streamed slowly up, against gravity.

The tumour was sweating and, shit, nobody obeyed the laws of physics anymore in my world.

I popped some chocolate pretzels because why not? Feeding a tumour is hard work and you need as much junk food as you can find.

A part of me knew this all had to be imaginary, but as each drop of sweat landed in the jug it splashed and tiny droplets landed on my skin. It was cold, and the temperature change was immediate. I knew I was going to have to deal with this at some point, but I was consumed with my writing. I would finish the damn book first, then have a nervous breakdown. I had stopped taking the fluoxetine because I ran out and didn't go back for a repeat prescription even though my saintly GP left several voicemails reminding me and telling me the dangers of abruptly stopping, which really wasn't true. Fluoxetine, of all of the drugs in its class, can be stopped abruptly because it's broken down into something called norfluoxetine, which stays in the blood for five days. Not that I was thinking of this at the time. I would have done the same if I had been on a different drug.

I did start to worry when the tumour seemed to move around from the corner of one eye to the other. It undulated, like a slug, and I worried about what its purpose might be. Or what it was growing into. I could still shape it, like a flesh sculpture, but that didn't affect its purpose. Or maybe I was the one directing it from my subconscious. That didn't help me because fuck knows what was going on in my mind at that time.

But I wrote. The words flowed like... tumour sweat, like the undulatory motion of a fleshy sculpture.

I didn't tell my boss any of this in the meeting.

'It must be stress,' I said.

'You're going to go to Occupational Health. You're going to be assessed for fitness to work,' he said.

'What? No,' I said. 'I'm fine. I've been working. There haven't been any complaints from my patients—'

'Actually...'

He produced a bunch of documents.

There had been complaints, but nebulous.

He looks scary. He looks like he's dying. He talks to himself. I've heard that psychiatrists are mad themselves, but this is ridiculous. He rushes off to the toilet so often. Does he have irritable bowel syndrome? He breaks off mid-sentence and can't find the train of thought anymore. He stinks. His hygiene has worsened considerably. Something is wrong. I think he is about to drop dead.

'When did these come in? They don't seem fair,' I said.

'I don't give a shit,' said my boss. That was uncharacteristic. He was a devout... something or the other. He didn't usually swear.

'Well, you should,' I said. 'Not a single one of these complaints is about the care they received.'

'Your appearance and the emotions you stimulate in them is part of the care. Get the all-clear from Occupational Health, Tade. It's the only way you're getting back to work. You stay away until then.'

'Fine, I will.'

I didn't.

14

Around the time I ate the last pages from the books given to me for research, Elise called me to the living room for a talk.

A reasonable person, Elise never holds a grudge. She acts, she does not brood.

'The advantage of taking action is you don't have to waste time and energy on sulking or stewing. It's healthier.'

She is the revenge type. You harm her or those she holds dear, she will do you damage, which is fine when you are not the object of her ire. I didn't like how she was staring at me and I didn't have Jessie Lightfoot for backup.

'I'm not going to ask you any questions,' she said. Her hands gripped the armrests of the chair tightly. She was stressed, but trying to look calm.

'All right.'

'I'm leaving. I'm taking Trap.'

Not ideal.

'Why?' I asked. Hint of a whine in my voice?

'Are you kidding?'

'I'm not. Why are you breaking up our marriage?'

'I'm not breaking it up. You are.'

'How? I don't want you to go anywhere. You're the one who's leaving.'

'Tade there's blood and shit all over your clothes. You disappear and can't be reached by phone. You don't say where you've been.'

'I'm working—'

'No, you're not.'

'Yes, I am. Just wait here.'

Fastest I had moved in a long time. I darted up the stairs, got my Moleskine, where I wrote my first drafts, and, out of breath, shoved it in Elise's face.

She opened it and read in silence. She flipped some pages. Her lips thinned.

'Is this a joke?' she asked.

'I know it's kind of raw, and uncomfortable, but that's what I've been working on. It's a first draft, so it's bound to look rough and ready. I know what you're thinking, and I think it's shocking, yes, but it touches an honesty—'

'What do you think you've written here?'

'A novella for the...'

I snatched it from her and flipped through because this was not the expected response or tone. I had thought she would be dazzled by my brilliant prose and all my eccentricities would fall away because they were in the service of art. True love would prevail, conquer all, as they say. Cue violins and movie credits.

Oh.

I saw it immediately.

'Um...'

'Yeah,' said Elise.

The book was full of prose, but it was the text of my last novel. They weren't bad words, in fact, there were flashes of brilliance, but they weren't new words and I had been regurgitating these for months, thinking I was writing pretentious studies for portraits.

'I'm confused...'

Elise got up. 'Yes, you are. You need to see someone, Tade, but I cannot let our son be exposed to this. I've not been up there but the stench from your study is overpowering. I honoured our agreement. Can you say you've been honourable?' She gave me room to respond, but I didn't take the bait. 'We're going to my mum's. Sort your shit out, Thompson.'

Alone in the house, I lived almost entirely in my study. The dripping of sweat from the ceiling into a basin became soothing. I got used to Lightfoot's absence. I didn't have to skulk around to wank when Henrietta got frisky anymore. I only visited the kitchen and the bathroom for my basic needs and to feed the sculpture.

But the writing. Since Elise had confronted me with what I was doing I hadn't been producing anything. The whole point of my research was to get a novel out of the experience. Bacon, in spite of his dissipations, always seemed to work. By all accounts he would spend the night carousing, get himself beaten up, go home, sleep it off or be fucked by some East End thug, wake up early and paint. That kind of discipline would be nice.

I wept. It was too much. My family, my medical practice, my literary ambitions, my health, all going or gone. I trembled with the emotion of it all. This transitioned to rigors and I may have had a fever.

Even the Destroyer rejected me.

'Jesus, go and have a bath and wear clean clothes. I told you, hygiene is number one and you smell like a tip. This is disrespectful. Get out.'

I couldn't smell myself, of course. I get my acute sense of smell from my mother. I think. She used to be able to tell when my stepfather had cheated by smelling other women on him. When I read

Perfume by Patrick Süskind I related to the main character instantly. Grenouille, the protagonist, clearly had a superpower and took olfaction to extremes, but for me the world was full of smells that spoke to me. In *Perfume* the ability was explored to its furthest possible ramifications. I can smell people. It's like people have olfactory signatures that I can identify. Nobody I knew had ever understood or, having attempted an understanding, believed me when I spoke of this. I thought everybody was like this when I was young. Body odours cause me pain and halitosis makes me run a mile.

To think I might be causing the same kind of discomfort to others made me ill and ashamed of myself. I went home, showered first, then ran a bath. I looked around for Elise's bath salt things. I didn't know bath salts so I just dumped a few in. They smelled like responsibility and leisure.

The quietness of the house got to me. This was just before Trap's bedtime and he would have been switching from one toy to the next, trying to get the maximum play time out of his waning wakefulness. Why kids' toys make such a racket I will never know. In his room the picture book he and I were drawing lay abandoned. I did think of finishing it in his absence, but then where would the father-son bonding be?

When I tired of the water I rose, sniffed my armpits and dried off. I avoided the mirror. I tried to straighten up my posture. After all, Destroyer couldn't see me. Muscles and ligaments had adjusted already, and they groaned with the effort, resisting. I would need exercise or physiotherapy, or both. I resumed slouching.

At the foot of the ladder, in the hallway, I stopped and took a deep breath.

Yeah, not a good experience. As I entered the attic, I saw the change immediately.

The flesh sculpture was in the middle of my psychic nest.

I knew this was real. Before, it was just in my visual field, but disappeared if I looked directly at it. This was the word made flesh, pulsating and heaving in the midst of chewed research material. I punched myself in the temple twice, blinked, squeezed my eyes shut. *Hello, Henrietta!* Opened them again, and the sculpture was still there.

The air was moist with its sweaty, yeasty odour; its pheromones and malignancy. I had to be sure; I had to touch it.

I inched forward, but my heart kept beating faster and faster the closer I got. I retreated and flew downstairs.

That thing had *hair*.

I didn't imagine that. The detail was too granular, and how did it get there? For one irrational moment I thought it was a prank. Elise wasn't above such things, but then again, she wasn't in the mood right now and I believed her when she said she hadn't been up.

I stared up at the attic door as if that would change anything. I half-expected the sculpture to rush down after me and I was aware of my nakedness. If this was America I'd have a .45 cocked and locked with thirteen rounds in the magazine and one in the chamber. I'd be ready to blast it, to kill anything. More likely I'd kill myself.

I'd played with a Glock before, but only once. Just after medical school I got this gig where I attended weapons testing in an army barracks in Nigeria. I did it for a month. The regular guy was off with plague or something (not hyperbole. The doctor had *yersinia pestis* and nobody could figure where he got it from since there was no local outbreak. Rumour had it the base was testing unauthorised biological weapons and while I like listening to conspiracy theories as folk storytelling, I could not fault this thinking). I was drafted in because the regulations required at least one physician on site when ordnance quality control activities were carried out. The army and their language, right?

The things I saw made me irritated at Hollywood films, particularly in the area of hand grenades. You know that casual way the hero pulls the pin and throws, taking his sweet time to get to cover? Trading quips? Saying something cool? Walking away in slo-mo, backing the explosion? None of that happened.

What did happen was a live grenade being handed to a fearful, trembling recruit with sweat on his brow and, if he was lucky, a flak jacket. He had to pull the pin, chuck the grenade down a hole and duck behind a concrete shield. By my estimation he had like two seconds to get to cover before the most god-awful blast flowered from the hole, scattering dust and stones everywhere, and leaving a ring in the ears despite the muffs provided. Explosives are a terrible thing. How did humanity evolve to this level of potential for carnage?

After I'd been there a week, I asked one of the COs if I could fire a gun, and he said sure and yanked out his sidearm. I think I knew the difference between a revolver and an automatic. His was the latter. I tried to rack the slide like they do in the movies. It was harder than I expected, or maybe this motherfucker didn't oil his gun. When I did manage to pull the slide back, it caught the web of flesh between my thumb and index finger, drawing blood. The soldiers laughed their heads off. I didn't hold a grudge because they were fun. They drank hard and made me jog with them and I treated their gonorrhoea. They told me stories of undeclared wars and extrajudicial assassinations. The world seemed darker to me, and when the old guy recovered and took his job back I was relieved.

Back in the UK a sales rep who was trying to sell me on a new psychiatric drug took me to see sniper rifles being tested at her husband's firm. I even fired one under heavily controlled conditions. I missed the target entirely.

This is all to say projectile weapons were never going to be part of my defence strategy, even if they were readily available in the UK, which they aren't unless you are a criminal or maybe a farmer.

Kitchen knives are the way to go. Get stabby.

I was going to do that but the phone rang. It was Elise.

'Your son wants to speak to you. Stand by,' she said, like a receptionist or phone operator. Cold, and barely maintaining civility because of Trap.

'Daddy?'

'Hey, Trap. How is Grandma?'

'She's making me dust her statues,' said Trap.

Elise's mum had these figurines of seventeenth-century folk from Amsterdam or some shit. They looked weird and always freaked Trap out.

'I'll let you in on a secret. If you break one of them she won't ask you to clean them anymore. Have you been drawing?'

'Yes. I drew in the toilet, but Grandma doesn't like it.'

'You can't draw on walls, Trap. We've told you that. When you get back we'll finish that picture book, okay?'

'When can I come home?'

'What did Mummy say?'

'That you weren't feeling well.'

No shit. 'She's right. I'm not.'

'Why can't we come and look after you?'

'Because I'm a doctor. I have superpowers that I'll use on myself.'

'Should I buy you some medicine?'

'Maybe later, Trap.'

'Daddy.'

'Yes?'

'Can you read me a story?'

I did.

Okay, no, I didn't. I only wrote that to make myself seem like a good dad. I did start to read him the story but my call waiting flashed and it was Destroyer. I told Trap I'd call him back. I never did.

Now you are judging me. Look, if this was an AA or NA story and I was reciting it in a meeting you'd forgive me. Try to think of me as some kind of addict, though I'm not sure what I was addicted to.

Destroyer had a few guests and had me over to serve drinks and clean up afterwards. It was midnight when she dismissed me. I walked home and had an idea on the way.

You know where to go in your neighbourhood, or at least you know where not to go, the places from which to steer your teenagers away. The front door is usually unstable from being broken in one too many times by police serving a warrant. The windows are usually boarded up. In the daytime, young folks slouch about or just sit on the stoop, eye-fucking passers-by. The place serves as a reservoir for petty criminals going out to get cash for a hit. Depends on the neighbourhood, of course. In some places it's a phone number. Rich folk don't like to deal with street-level suppliers on the actual street. I had a doctor friend in the 90s who had a heroin habit. He used from Friday evening to Sunday night. On Monday morning he smoked crack, which countered any somnolence. Then he'd take risperidone, which he also got from his dealer in Shepherds Bush, for the paranoia. He seemed okay. In the 90s, at least. In 2006 he got caught stealing antipsychotics from the patients' tray in the hospital and I haven't heard from him since.

But here was me, at one am, at *that* house.

At some point a family must have loved this house enough to pay the mortgage. Right now it looked like a strong wind could blow it to Kansas. Moss on the ground crawling up the sides and some species of wild ivy climbing up its walls made it seem like nature was trying to reclaim it. There were some sounds from inside, and through a crack in the window I saw people playing dice with periodic cheers and groans. Music waxed and waned.

There was a guy sitting at the door and he stretched out his hand for an entrance fee. Though blanketed in shadow, he was large. I wondered if he was the kind of large that never had to prove himself in a fight. I'd fought larger guys before. It could go either way, but the strategy is expect to get hit, try not to get hit in the head, try to hit back more times with greater accuracy, and be ruthless. Don't hesitate. My instructor said to conduct each fight as if your life is in danger.

But I didn't want to fight this guy.

'I'm not here for that,' I said.

'Then scram, innit?' he said.

'I need you to do something. I'll give you money.'

I handed him forty quid, which is all I had on me.

'What do you need?' he asked.

'I want you to beat me up.'

Okay, this was more like it.

When you get hit by a person who knows how to punch, you have an out-of-body experience. A proper swing to the gut doesn't just take your breath away. Done right, it makes your intestines go into spasm, and if you've had a recent meal, you'll think of vomiting. A hit to the face blooms like fireworks behind the eyes, a pleasant brightness cut short when the pain arrives, even if nothing is broken. You can hear a pure tone, low-volume ringing in the ears. Temple, eye, nose, angle of the jaw, hit, hit, hit, hit. These places can so incapacitate you that your limbs become flesh noodles.

This was familiar. Everything else, my life experience, my medical practice, my wife, my son, my life, was all a farce. A good farce, but no less of a performance. My entire existence anticipated this, waiting for something to go wrong, waiting for the next beating from my mother or my stepfather or my father. In this pain, in this suffering, which could not have lasted longer than five minutes, I was home. I was where I belonged. I finally understood the purity of Bacon's masochism.

And, fuck, I had to go to hospital because I pissed blood.

I told them I had been mugged. No, I didn't want to press charges. Yes, it was appalling how the police had been defunded. We needed bobbies on the street, yes? No, there's nobody to call, just patch me up.

Catheter through my penis to my bladder, draining the urine into a transparent bag, which I could stare at. Maybe my kidney was bruised, they couldn't tell just yet. I would have to spend the night, get some scans, rest, take some high-potency painkillers.

I ate that abominable hospital jelly and watched *The Bridge on the River Kwai* before nodding off.

I woke up with a start at four am, thinking of Trap and the incomplete bedtime story.

Oops.

15

Elise wasn't taking my calls.

Not that I blamed her, but on the bright side she hadn't mentioned the D word and I was in the mood to count my blessings.

The day after a beating is the most painful. Your endorphins abandon you and, like I mentioned before, the cute little nervelets that are growing back rupture easily. Here I went on a long digression about the nature of pain, its neurophysiology and psychology. The editor made me cut it as irrelevant. Editors are hell beasts who suck the life out of art and spit out bland, inoffensive pap because they are convinced that's what readers want.

Anyway.

I was in pain. I couldn't climb up to the attic to check on the sculpture. I tried to phone my wife a number of times. Failure. I found a loose filling. My piss was suspiciously dark, but no more blood, so there was that.

Destroyer called. I stared at the ringing phone for some seconds and decided to ignore it. This was a breach of our contract. I had agreed to always pick up the phone, no matter what the circumstances. Well. Circumstances. I drank water to flush out my kidneys and bladder. The pain was such that I couldn't even respond to Henrietta when I closed my eyes. Cured at last?

I had one black eye on the left. I lay down on the sofa and played the audiobook of *Fear and Loathing in Las Vegas*. Not because of the content, which I loved with a burning hot passion. No, I listened to this particular audiobook obsessively because of the narrator. Ron McLarty's voice is soothing to me. I almost had an accident driving to Birmingham from Thamesmead because I put one of the discs on and dozed off. Just for a second, but I swerved and I had a moment of *this is how you die, Thompson*, but I corrected and parked immediately.

I sank into Hunter S. Thompson's gonzo, stream-of-consciousness reportage. Here too was a guy on an assignment and nobody edited *his* irrelevant digressions. Barbra Streisand paintings, bats, apes being attracted to water and biting the faces off folks, lizard people, gigantic Samoans and Margaret fucking Mead.

Mead is well-known for *Coming of Age in Samoa* which purports to describe… I don't know, sexual behaviour and shit among young Samoans. I lived in Samoa for two years and that book is a crock of utter bollocks. There is one basic thing you need to know about Samoa and Samoans: friendliness, harmony and pleasing people, particularly visitors, is more important than truth, whatever truth is. It's more important to keep the person you're talking to happy than it is to be factual. You learn that in a week. Also, you learn to carry rocks or a cane around with you if you're not driving because of the roving gangs of feral dogs. Sticks and stones, baby. You throw rocks, they leave you alone.

I don't know if HST intended the juxtaposition of Mead and his Samoan attorney Dr Gonzo, but it might be one of those 'accidents' that Bacon talked about in the creation of his paintings. Oscar Zeta Acosta, the guy HST based Dr Gonzo on, was definitely not Samoan, and disappeared in Mexico in 1974, presumed dead. He was a Chicano activist but also not averse to drug use, so who knows if he was murdered?

Demon editor removed a long digression on the Chicano Movement, blaming your attention span and the fact that I was showing off. I'm not bitter.

McLarty lured me into a deep sleep not unaided by opiates. I woke up four hours later, refreshed, still in agony, and with a dead phone. I plugged it in and boiled water for spaghetti. Outside the kitchen window a cat lingered. I called him Bob and he had a collar, so he belonged to someone, but does anybody really own cats? I got one of Trap's old plastic bowls and tipped in tuna from a can. I went outside, groaned like an old man, and gave the offering to Bob. I had no idea if Bob was a male or female and I don't know if you can sex cats from a distance. I do know that they're supposed to like fish. Bob ate the tuna which the container announced had been sourced humanely, another way of saying no dolphins were harmed in the fishing process, which is apparently a thing. Elise is the tuna person. I can't stand it myself. The flesh seems water-logged, and the texture is off.

We did have a cat once when I was a kid. A kitten. Again, I didn't know the sex. The kitten got itself entangled in some twine and strangulated. It wasn't the first dead animal I ever saw, but it was the first that I had an emotional connection with. There was a blackout the night we found it.

The phone beeped a number of times, messages coming in.

I pieced together this from the Destroyer over several texts:

'Hi. How are you feeling? I'm really sorry, Tade. I don't think I've been fair to you or treated you with kindness. I like you and I think you're a decent person, but I would be lying to you if I said you were all right. You have problems. We all have problems, but yours are new and raw. I don't believe you anymore. I don't believe you are researching a novel. I don't believe your time with me is "Participant Observation" like you put it. This is a spiral and it won't end well.

Seek treatment. I am fond of you, you know? And when you're better, after your treatment, you have my number. But I can't enable what seems to be self-harm. You're a shrink, you should know this. Please message me back and tell me if you're okay.'

Where did art end and self-harm begin? When my sex worker asked me to get help? The Destroyer was turning into a cliché, a Heart of Gold moment. Whoever writes real life needs new ideas. I was touched, though. My instinct was to pick up the phone and ask her if she loved me. You have to understand that those of us brought up without maternal love sometimes have difficulties with affection signals. Any nurturing goes into that black hole where Mother's love was meant to be. It is never enough. The yearning for some kind of appreciation means what is normal human compassion takes on romantic proportions. Rejection is monumental. Our defence mechanism kung fu is transcendent and I am a master. I would reject anybody before they inevitably rejected me. Smooth.

I didn't message Destroyer back. I edited her name to DON'T PICK UP and discontinued the standing order that paid her. It felt like a break-up. Why did it feel like a break-up?

I wanted to write. I had notebooks downstairs and I emailed an old accountability buddy of mine in Wisconsin. I asked if he wanted to word bank with me, like the old days when we were both beginners. He had remained a dabbler, but he was diligent, which is what I needed. I also needed eyes that were not mine glancing over what I was writing to ensure it was new stuff, not a Xerox of an earlier novel.

I wrote for an hour, transcribed and emailed it without revision to Wisconsin Guy.

I felt depleted. Lightfoot hadn't come back and Henrietta had become ineffective. In agony I climbed up to the attic, sure that I would lose my footing, fall and break my fucking neck any minute.

The sculpture was rising and falling, like it was breathing. I should have brought a broom to prod it with. Was it still feeding on my flesh?

I screamed at it. Briefly at first, then in a prolonged shriek. I don't know what I was expecting, but it didn't respond. I took a deep breath then screamed again and again until I started seeing purple spots. I sat down, surrounded by this musky miasma coming from it. The good news was it had no teeth or any means of harming me that I could see. I had to get rid of the sculpture, but no way was I going to touch it. The slime that covered it, the sweat that dripped from it, the wavelike motion, all triggered my gag reflex. I thought of hiring someone, but they might call the RSPCA or the police. Not good. The police were blunt instruments at the best of times. If they saw something they didn't understand they would arrest first, make sense of it later. I've been to the cells before and it was unpleasant even as a visitor.

I couldn't do anything while I was in pain, so I descended again, physically from the attic and metaphorically into pharmaceuticals.

All the screaming tired me out so I took a nap. I woke up with more pain so I took some codeine and sloshed rum in my mouth and went back to sleep. Kids, don't mix opiates with alcohol. Don't try this at home. I am a professional degenerate, so I can get away with this.

I either slept for four hours or lost time. I did not dream, but I woke up with a burning idea. I pushed all the furniture out of the way in the sitting room. I went to the back yard. There were two bicycles, Elise's and Trap's. I haven't ridden since a 2003 race across the Thames where I disgraced myself.

Also in the yard, a punching bag on a chain attached to a stand.

I leapt into the garage, found a saw, came back out and cut both bicycle frames until I had ten poles. I dismantled the punching bag stand and laid out the frame. A little wobbly, but it might work.

I've had duct tape handy since I saw that they used it to seal the hole in the International Space Station in 2018. I took all the bits of metal and piled them on the carpet. Next I swept through the house looking for boxes of all kinds.

I'm slightly arty. I draw with ink and brush. Pastels, sometimes. I paint with acrylics and oils. Apart from the abomination upstairs, I haven't done any sculpture, except, you know, craft with the child.

It was more difficult than I had thought and I used up all the duct tape in the house, but I finally had it.

It doddered, and a sneeze would probably bring it down, but I had a large cage in the living room. I laid thin strips of cardboard, some hanging down from the top like a curtain, others all around the floor radiating outwards. I dragged a chair from the dining table and situated it in the middle of the cage, then sat on it. Not right. I closed all the windows and shut the door. Dimness, a gloom bordering on darkness since it was so late.

Still not right. I zipped upstairs, hurting and creaking as I went, and I rifled through the wardrobe. I couldn't find anything purple, so I took whatever was closest to that on the visual spectrum. Draped in one of Elise's dresses, I sat on the chair in the middle of the cage. The opiates started to catch up with me after the frenzy of activity and I yawned so hard, my mouth so wide, I feared dislocating my jaw.

I yelled at the top of my voice with my lungs as full as I could get them.

Like before, again and again and again.

When I was tired, and my lids were so heavy, I found myself pregnant with words and I had to get them down before—

Doorbell.

Before you get to the next part, I maintain this was not my fault.

I urgently wanted to write down the words in my forebrain.

It was the police at the door.

'Do you live here, sir?' asked the guy, a constable, fresh-faced, white, earnest.

I looked beyond him. A cop car at the kerb, older guy inside. Him I knew from my community work, although I couldn't tell if he recognised me or not. Nobody else on the street, although I imagined my neighbours listening with directional mics and other espionage-grade equipment. Credit where it's due, no curtains seemed to flutter or roll back.

'Sir?' said the constable. He looked worried and did he wrinkle his nose?

'Yes, I live here. What's the problem, officer?' In a voice that said, fuck you.

Fuck you, because Sir Edward Coke said so.

For a man's house is his castle, et domus sua cuique est tutissimum refugium *(and each man's home is his safest refuge).*

But I didn't say that because I didn't want this guy in my house.

'What's your name, sir?'

I told him.

'We received reports of an altercation from this address. Sounds of loud distress.'

'What does loud distress sound like, officer?'

'Shouting, sir.'

'I see.'

'Do you mind if we come in and look around?'

'Do you mind if I see a warrant first?'

'We'll be quick. Just to be sure everyone's okay. Is there anyone else in the house?'

'Okay, listen. I do not have to tell you any fucking thing. I don't have to answer your questions. I don't know what you're expecting to find, but you can show me a warrant or get the fuck off my property.'

'There's no call for that kind of language, sir.' He cocked his head. 'Have you been in a fight, sir?'

'Is this any of your business?'

I have no idea why I was being so combative. Okay, I do. I fucking hated the police. Remember way back when I told you my brother and I had to steal food when my father was detained? Well, the police held him without trial, seized his assets, and froze his bank accounts for eighteen months, and when there was no evidence of any offence they released him. He took them to court the next day and after like ten years, he won the case. They never paid the damages. My father died. They did not pay his estate either.

There was and is no reason to talk to the police. They even *have* to tell you that you don't have to talk to them. Most people, even fucking crims, think being entangled in the criminal justice system is the time to get it all off their chest. It really isn't. Any involvement with the police is the time to make like a monk and shut the fuck up. Make them work for everything and give nothing away, even if you haven't done anything, because they'll take what you say in jest or by mistake and create a felony out of it.

None of which was this sweet boy's fault, but he wore the uniform. The thin blue line is the cyanosed lips of an oxygen-starved victim of police brutality.

Older guy came out, all placatory good cop and ting. Babylon.

I banished them both with crisp consonants and middle-class outrage, promising to keep the noise down. I wasn't sure it would work until it did.

I fell asleep in the hallway, on the floor, in what I was wearing.

I woke up to knocking again. It was bright, but I was discombobulated for a minute, and Henrietta wasn't helping.

'I told you to get a warrant,' I said, so groggy, I couldn't work the lock.

When I got the door open, Destroyer was standing there.

'Oh, thank god. I thought you were dead,' she said, concern furrowing her brow.

She looked different, conservative. Blouse, jacket, jeans, hair tightly controlled, an office worker.

'How are you here?' I asked. 'How do you know where I live?'

'I know where all my clients live, Tade. Due diligence. It's best not to wake up murdered, don't you think?'

Not being murdered was best.

'Okay. Why are you here? I've stopped the standing order, and as per the contract, that means no service.'

'Are you going to invite me in?'

'I suppose I'd better,' I said. I moved back and she walked in. Her shoes click-clacked on the panelling.

'Did you sleep in those clothes?' she asked.

'I did, right where you're standing.'

She touched my swollen face. 'What happened to you?'

'Why does everybody want to know?' I pulled away. 'I don't want to go into it, all right? Why are you here? My family lives here.'

She looked up and around. 'Really? Because you're not whispering, and you let me in.'

I needed my codeine fix and she was in the way. 'Get to the point. I have a busy day ahead.'

'I just wanted to be sure you were okay. And you left this at my place.'

She handed me a Batman key-pendant. Trap had given it to me on my last birthday. I always made sure I had it with me, but I hadn't thought of it in ages. Broke off my keys, most likely, but the shitty thing was how I didn't notice its absence.

Destroyer hugged me and it was surprisingly warm. I was ready to surrender to her then, just sink in and relax. Forget everything that might be—

Key in lock, wiggle round, door opened.

Elise.

16

The guy took a drag of his cigarette and placed it on the windowsill, a line of smoke reaching from the lit end to the ceiling.

'You don't remember me, do you?' he asked. He busied himself wrapping filthy torn clothes around his knuckles.

'I was here one night weeks ago,' I said.

He shook his head. 'Before that. A year ago, year and a half. Victoria Station. You took my cat.'

'Oh, that was you?'

'Yes,' he said, and punched me in the jaw. New pain, plus old pain reignited.

The Victoria Station Cat. Shit, I remembered that.

The police called up about this homeless guy who they said was mentally unwell. So two doctors, myself and some other guy who wore leather and rode a souped-up muscle car in London where such things are useless, turned up to assess this guy and decide if he was going to be detained under the Mental Health Act. Muscle Car Guy is dead now, by the way. Car accident.

The homeless gentleman wasn't mentally unwell, just really high on amphetamines, which meant he could be taken away temporarily.

What nobody told us is that he had this tabby. Most homeless people who had pets that I had seen up to that point had dogs.

This was the first one with a cat. Don't ask me how, but it became my role to wait at Victoria Station for the fucking RSPCA and they took their sweet time. This cat, who I was reliably informed was called Serpico, did not go easily. She ruined my £400 coat, scratched me and earned me weird looks from commuters who thought I was trying to steal this stray cat to sacrifice it to Satan, or some shit. When I tell this story I usually say it took two hours for the RSPCA person to arrive, but it seemed longer.

Turns out Serpico didn't make it back to her owner.

He decided to take it out on me, and not just because I paid him fifty bucks to beat the shit out of me. What happened next was entirely his fault.

Obviously, I was still annoyed about the coat and the scratches and my wasted time. I mean, he couldn't have known that, but he could have just kept quiet and beaten me more. I didn't have to know he had a grudge.

When he swung at me I slipped it and countered with a right hook, sending him right to the ground. He landed with a wet, smacking sound.

'Ah, shit. Sorry, sorry, it was a reflex. I don't know what came over me.'

I do. My training kicked in and I did not stop it.

His lip was bloody and it looked to me like he would have a black eye soon. He got up, got his legs back, wiped his mouth with the back of his hand.

'You know, I thought you was a grass when you first walked up.'

'Again, really sorry. I'm not with the police. Let's continue our arrangement.'

He proceeded and I was impressed at his professionalism. He didn't strike me in the kidneys once because I told him about my hospital visit. Such a gentleman.

My one claim to fame has been knocking out an Olympic taekwondo hopeful back in university. My club had been grooming this one guy, training him for weeks, one-to-one work with the sabonim. I had never really gone all out because at the time I had no idea what medical specialty I would be pursuing. I had to protect my hands in case I decided to become a surgeon.

As part of the final week for the preparation before the trials, they brought me in to spar with this guy, probably expecting him to make short work of me. We got into the square, bowed and started. He darted all over the space, wasting energy, trying to distract me or something, I don't know. The strategy was opaque to me. I stayed in the centre, still, turning around to keep up with where he was. He closed quickly to kick me. I sidestepped into him and slammed him in the centre of the chest with a side kick, full power, fully anchored. I can't swear to it, but I think it lifted him off his feet a little. He fell, unconscious. Shit, I thought I had killed him. I hadn't.

Everyone was quiet, but I knew what they were thinking.

Why aren't we taking Tade to the Olympics?

It wasn't because I was hot shit. It was because the guy underestimated me. It wasn't a lucky kick, but if he had been more serious I wouldn't have been able to knock him out.

And if this guy working out on me had been smarter, he wouldn't have pissed me off and ended up on the floor.

But you want to know what happened with Elise meeting Destroyer, don't you?

It is a curious thing that electricity that passes between human beings, that aliveness that is communicated by locking your attention on another and knowing that the other's attention is locked on you. All senses funnel to that pinpoint focus. It doesn't matter if it's love or hate that underlies the look, it makes the subject feel special.

At first I could not parse the look they exchanged, although the emotional currents were fairly straightforward. Here was a strange woman in Elise's space, in her home, with her husband. Not in flagrante delicto, but might as well have been. In those first few seconds of sizzling stares, anything could have happened. Destroyer could have been a Jehovah's Witness. That wouldn't have been an unreasonable assumption to make. I had been known, when bored, to invite them into the house just to engage in a theological argument. One has to hone the skills of rhetoric somehow. Elise always knew when I was looking for verbal conflict as sport and tuned out. Trap was too young. Nobody understood that when you grew up with a lawyer like my dad who also undoubtedly had some kind of personality disorder, your debating game had to be tight. Everything from an extra portion of pork chops to an increment in pocket money was at stake. I had to make a case for everything. Imagine my surprise at the real world when I found out this wasn't routine and that the ability to argue didn't get you friends. It made me tedious and difficult to deal with. Humans avoid people who are tedious and difficult to deal with, and if you combine that with my already fractious upbringing, I wasn't growing up to be the life of the party. I could fake it for a night or two at a soiree, but I couldn't live it. Most people stayed away from me, which is one of the reasons nobody checked on me while this Francis Bacon malarkey was happening.

Elise said, 'I'm going to have some tea.'

Other women would have asked who Destroyer was, and although Elise would have wanted to know, she would never condescend to give the slightest advantage by asking for anything, even basic information. When it came to being offended, she was a scorched-Earth kind of person. She slid through into the house leaving me and Destroyer standing there.

'Oops,' said Destroyer, in a small voice, a whisper practically. She hunched and shrunk herself, much in the same way she commanded me to. I realised that this was a submission display for Elise who wasn't there to see it. 'I'm glad you're alive. I'd better go.'

I let her leave, but didn't say anything. I was emotional and didn't trust the words that might have poured out. Seriously, I might have said I loved her just because she came to check on me, even though by so doing she had probably taken dynamite to my marriage. My heart was that hungry. My psychotherapist, the one who told me that I was well-defended, said I was a hungry ghost, preta in Buddhism, and that this tendency would come out at times of stress. She was right, I was, and it did. But I hid it well in most situations.

'She's pretty,' said Elise when I got back into the house. 'Legs the way you like them.' She was drinking from a mug standing at the counter in the kitchen.

'She's—'

Elise held up a hand. 'I don't care who she is, Tade.'

'It's not—'

'It is exactly what I think.'

'What is it that you think?'

'That you brought a whore into our house. Did you fuck her in our bed?'

'What? I would never—'

'Stop, stop, stop. You don't get to say what you would never do.'

That was true, actually. By that time I had no idea what I was capable of. The needle on my moral compass was spinning out of control.

'How much did you pay her?' asked Elise.

She was going to find out anyway, so I told her.

'Jesus, Tade.'

'I know it sounds bad, but it was for research. I swear. The insight is invaluable. I'm writing this incredible thing.'

'I'm sure that made sense in your head. Did the words make sense to you after they came out of your mouth?'

'Art can be—'

'Are you justifying cheating by blaming art?'

'I wasn't cheating,' I said, but that sounded hollow. 'Not exactly.'

'What the hell does "not exactly" mean? What were you paying for?'

'I didn't fuck her. She fucked me. So that I could understand Francis Bacon.'

'Sorry, what are you... how?'

'With a dildo.'

'What?'

'He was gay.'

'I know Francis Bacon was gay, you idiot. What makes you think getting sodomised by a big-breasted, long-legged cunt-whore hooker is the same thing?'

Since we're being honest here, my first instinct was to point out her tautology. That was just how my brain handled distress. The second instinct was to realise that she was right. I had been doing it wrong. I was still clinging to my heterosexual schema for safety. Justifications. It was a woman penetrating me, therefore it wasn't gay? I wasn't penetrating her, therefore it wasn't (really) cheating? No wonder I was stuck.

'Hey!' said Elise. 'Focus! Where are you? Your eyes look glazed.'

'I—'

'Show it to me,' she said.

'Show what?'

'What you've written. This book that is so important you'd destroy your family over it.'

'I don't want to until I get the first draft out of—'

'I don't care if you want to or not. You showed me what you

thought was the previous draft anyway. Let's see it. Now, Tade.'

I emailed her the stuff I had sent to Wisconsin and stood there while she read it on her phone. I really needed my next dose of opioids by this time.

'Tade, this person climbing up trees in Africa is meant to be me?'

I nodded. 'What you're reading are portraits of people, studies for portraits in the way that Bacon titled... It has to reflect truth.'

'What the fuck are you talking about? I've never been to Africa. This never happened to me.'

Wait.

Wait. What?

'Who are you writing about?'

At first I thought she was whispering, but the blood rushing through my head had got louder.

'Tade, look at me. Who do you see?'

I looked up.

Study of...

Portrait of...

Fuck it.

This is what I saw.

A tall woman, taller than me at any rate. Brown hair, green eyes, long face, pale complexion. Huh.

'Who do you see?'

A black woman, dark as roiling pitch, gigantic Afro, skinny like a stick insect, angular face, red lips.

'Who do you see?'

Henrietta Moraes.

And that's about the time when I left home. It was just like when I ran away without planning it. Strangely, I used the survival techniques I learned from homeless people that I had assessed in the past. Hang around the back of supermarkets and eat the food they discard.

I wasn't really homeless, but I spent a few days on the street. When you can't even see the wife in front of you it's time to get some distance and re-evaluate.

Who was Elise? That was what I spent the days wondering and different images flashed through my head as I wandered to my crack house and asked my guy to beat the shit out of me again. Apart from me punching him to the ground, it was going well. Each hit I received helped empty my mind. I wanted oblivion.

I didn't really come for the beating. I came because of what Elise said about Destroyer. This had been on my mind since then, and when he went panting to his seat and resumed his cigarette, I croaked from where I lay.

'What?' he said.

'Rent boy,' I said.

'You're surprising, doc.'

'Can you get one?'

No need, he told me. He could provide this service. Extra, of course.

In that dank, dilapidated building, he took the role of an anonymous male sex worker and sodomised me with the help of one latex condom and copious amounts of olive oil, which I'm told is not good with rubbers.

At least Destroyer had prepared me somewhat. When it was over I didn't feel particularly different or any closer to understanding Bacon. Turns out gay sex is just like hetero sex on the emotional front at least. Lightning didn't strike me down. That was always a possibility because even though I claim not to believe in God, I still think he's there from time to time, and I expect him to chastise me when I fuck up. And his servants say gay sex is a no-no. Assholes.

I went back to hospital to the shaking heads of ED nurses who could tell that this harm was, at least partially, self-inflicted. They patched me up, asked if I wanted to see psych, to which I laughed, but not maniacally. The last thing I wanted was to get detained under the Mental Health Act, which, heh, is hilarious considering what was in store for me. I left hospital and I went home. It was midday and on a working day, so nobody was there. I was in pain, but used to it, and I wanted writing materials.

Pain, undiluted, is a great motivator and I wanted to capture that unsoiled reality before it leached away.

I noticed that my Volvo wasn't in the driveway. I didn't know if Elise had it towed or if someone had stolen it. Not in my neighbourhood. But I was bringing the place down by just existing. Whoremonger and sodomite, as the holy book says.

I burst into uncontrollable tears without warning. Fucking use a segue, Thompson. Non-sequiturs don't work. This is not Goddard.

I sat in the cage in my living room, sobbing. I wasn't even sad. It made no sense at all to me, and emotions are my day job. I dry swallowed some opioids and climbed into the attic.

I couldn't smell anything because my nostrils were dressed and I was mouth-breathing. The flesh sculpture had grown, and rose and fell like bellows. It looked like a giant's scrotum. That was probably one of those To a Hammer Everything Looks Like a Nail things.

I got a cleaver and knives from the kitchen, returned and went into a frenzied stabbing spree.

17

I once had a book plagiarised.

Not passages from the book, the entire book. Some guy in Latvia or some other Baltic state slapped his name on one of my science fiction novels and passed it off as his own. Did book tours and shit, got lauded for being able to write the authentic black African experience. How did he do that, interviewers asked. How did he, a lily-white Baltic-state dude with that soft, silky hair they have, how did he get into the mind of an African.

There are these gatherings called science fiction conventions, where guys like me and people from all over the world come together to celebrate all our nerdiness. Ever since Hollywood decided to use our books as source material the gatherings have been big, expensive affairs with corporate sponsorship.

Conventions have a particular and replicated anthropology. You have the convention hotel, which is either the same building as the convention, connected to the convention centre or close to the convention centre, so that attendees can just walk over to the activities. Rooms at the hotel go fast because people usually come from different countries and daily transport costs can add to your expenses and reduce the amount of time you have to hang out. Cinderella pumpkin rules. You have your convention committee, a bunch of dedicated volunteers who care about science fiction more than you ever will. They usually staff the registration desk where you will be recognised, stamped, ID'd, handed a goody bag and directed to your first activity.

To a stranger it will seem like a shit ton of people just milling about in an open space, but it's highly organised if you know what to look for. Those people in outlandish or landish costumes? They're the cosplayers. Do not touch them. Do not take photographs of them without permission. Do say hello and ask them questions.

There's a map to tell you where to go for each activity.

And there's a dealer's room, where artists, writers, gamers and other purveyors of geeky stuff are allowed to display and sell their wares.

That's how I found out about this motherfucker. He'd brought with him a shit ton of copies of the book so he could sign and sell them. He had posters and flyers, which is one of the reasons I was angry: he had more cool stuff than my publishers would shell out for, the fuckers.

We recognised each other immediately, him from my face, me from watching him exchange a book with my title on it for money.

'Motherfucker!' I yelled, charging him. I didn't know what I was going to do when I got to his stall. Rugby tackle him? I had no plan.

He leapt up and rabbited. My momentum propelled me right into his corner and I took a spill along with all his cool merch and the plagiarised books. I scrambled up and went after him.

'Stop!'

He ran out of the convention centre on to the streets of... I still want to say Latvia, but who the fuck knows? I gave chase. Again, I had no idea why. I didn't speak the language, I didn't know the streets, I was just angry.

I chased him across a playground, through some graffiti-decorated alleyway, past a pharmacy where he changed direction and ran across the road, weaving his way through oncoming traffic. Which I also did and almost got pureed by Latvian vehicles. I'm pretty sure I got racially abused by drivers, but I might just be imagining it.

By this time my body complained. I hadn't run for months. My heart was the most vocal. *Why the fuck are you running, Thompson? Are you hunting? Gathering? Didn't we evolve to run on soft surfaces, and not concrete? Stop running right now!*

Luckily, Yanuz Yeltsin, which is the nom de plume this motherfucker chose, was about as fit as I was. That is to say, as fit as a typical writer. Which is to say, not fit at all. The job requires sitting on your arse all day and exercising by making pots of tea. Conducive to middle-age spread.

Yanuz stopped on a park bench, bent over, wheezing, hands dangling near his feet. He had a bald spot on the crown of his head. I plopped down next to him, gasping, trying to catch my breath which I left a mile behind me.

We caught each other's eyes and got the giggles. You can never tell what that electricity between humans will do from one moment to the next. We laughed as if we were at an unfunny comedy club but needed to get our money's worth. He laughed until he cried. I laughed until I started coughing.

'Let me buy you a coffee,' said Yanuz.

'Lay on, Macduff,' I said, muscles aquiver.

'What does this mean, lay on?'

'Let's go.'

We sat down across from each other. Every single person seemed to be blonde. Not even a smattering of black folks for me to nod to.

Yanuz was an amiable fellow, I found. Well known about town too. He knew a lot of the people in the coffee shop by name.

'I come here to write,' he said. 'It's nice.'

'Where is your own writing? Why did you steal my book?'

'I'm sorry,' he said, and he sounded and looked genuine. 'Listen. If I take you to a bookshop you will see in the science fiction section Stephen King, Isaac Asimov, Ursula Le Guin, Robert Heinlein. You know these, yes.'

'Of course.'

'These will be in English or translation. Do you know how many local authors get science fiction book deals?'

'No.'

'None. Not one. The best you can hope for is to self-publish. And no budget for publicity.'

'I see.'

'I don't think you do. I have wanted to be a writer since I was five. I have never wanted to be anything else, and I have never wanted to write anything else except science fiction. I know my work is good, and I have put in the hours and the training. Why should that disadvantage me in my own fucking country, eh, Thompson?'

'Call me Tade.'

'So I translated your book and called it my own, and translated it back to English for the "international edition". In a limited sense, I get to live my dream. In a limited sense.'

I went home with him and met his partner. I read some of his short stories, which were quite good. I missed my activities at the convention when Yanuz and I went drinking that night. I met some of his other writer friends who were in the same plight.

I have a copy of the plagiarised book, signed by Yanuz Yeltsin. I framed it and if I look up and to the left from where I'm writing this, I can see it clearly.

Yanuz's story made me maudlin, but he and I still correspond. I didn't report him to my publishers because, like I said, amiable guy. How can you grass on someone you've shared beers with? Someone whose partner made you coffee? And, holy of holies, who shared an unedited manuscript with you? Nah, Yanuz was okay.

One of the topics Yanuz and I chopped around was how to dispose of a body. Writers talk about this kind of thing all the time, and not because we're morbid assholes, which we certainly can be if you look at our search history. We have to write believable stories about murder sometimes, though it can't be so realistic that the book becomes a manual for potential murderers. I seem to recall Chuck Palahniuk including the recipes for bombs in his books but changing one or two ingredients. You have to have verisimilitude, though. The reader has to believe that in the world you create, it would work.

Yanuz said the key ingredient was patience. You have your dead guy or gal, and you have your deep freezer. You calm the fuck down, you remove all the food from your freezer. You chop the body up and freeze the bits. You wait twenty-four hours. While waiting you use a random number generator to put pins in the map, as many pins as you have body parts. You travel to those spots over days, and drop the parts. Easy.

And so, following my Latvian plagiarist's advice, I chopped the flesh sculpture up into sixteen pieces. It wasn't hard after my earlier stabbing spree. Each piece throbbed and pulsed. It didn't bleed a lot, but there was slime everywhere, making it difficult to grip the hatchet. Like when you chop up a snail to cook. In Nigeria you use a flocculant to clean off the slime, usually alum or aluminium sulphate. I didn't have any of that. It was a slippery, smelly job.

I discarded all the food and froze the parts of the sculpture.

The smell lingered in the study, but my olfaction wasn't yet back to normal, so it was fine. I wrote and transcribed and determined a calendar for dropping bits of the flesh. I sent my words to Wisconsin. I needed a nap so I lay in the middle of the nest, where the sculpture had been, and I curled up, floating on a codeine haze. I dreamt of mechanical dragonflies and sticky viscous sweat-rain.

I took the first chunk of flesh sculpture, wrapped it up, dropped it in my bag and left the house for my first destination. It was far away, so I took the tube. I sat with it on the floor between my legs, muscles rigid with tension. Everybody seemed to be staring at me. Sweat tracked down from my armpits.

The train shuddered to a stop between stations. The lights flickered.

'Ladies and gentlemen, we'll be staying here for some time. There is a fault. I'll inform you when I know more. I do apologise.'

I thought it would probably be for a few minutes, but we were there for an hour during which time the carriage got hotter, and that which was frozen became warm and went soft again.

This fucking thing. Didn't bleed much when I cut it, started gushing blood now. The floor between my legs was a red puddle and even I, with my broken nose, got that abattoir smell.

People were definitely staring this time.

I would probably have got away with it, but I had a sense of guilt. Why, though? I had stabbed and dismembered a product of my own imagination. At most, I had broken some social convention around the transportation of meat in public places. It wasn't human. True, I made a mess, but is that any different from vomiting on the tube after a night on the piss?

When the train started moving again I stood up, blood dripping from my bag, eyes following me everywhere. I waited at the door and when we arrived at a station I couldn't mind the gap fast enough. I clutched the bag to my chest like a sick child, earning more looks and being so deranged that crowds parted for me like the Red Sea for Moses, although I may be mixing both plagues and metaphors.

Transport police were waiting at the top of the escalator. They were polite, so there was that. They whisked me away, although they did not arrest me or read me my rights.

Gaddamn Babylon. Don't talk to them.

'What's in the bag?'

The inevitable question. At least I still had my wits about me, or enough wits to remember my own advice: shut the fuck up.

'What's your name, sir?'

'What's in the bag?'

'Are you all right? You look a little banged up.'

'What's your name, sir?'

'You know we'll test the contents of the bag?'

'Do you need medical attention?'

'What's your name, sir?'

Shut the fuck up, Thompson.

'The bag's in the lab. You'll put yourself in a position of advantage if you just tell us what it is, sir. Get ahead of this thing. It counts towards leniency.'

'What's your name, sir?'

'You know, I looked at it before we sent it to the pathology lab. It looked cut. Had it been cut?'

Pathology lab. I did some pathology. I did it for about a month before I decided I would rather work with living human beings. For one thing, pathologists, I mean medical pathologists now, are the single most boring group of medical specialists there are. At least psychiatrists have the reputation of being crazy. Pathologists are in black and white, although a few are in greyscale. I struggled to stay awake in the team meetings.

And you'd never believe the shit people brought to us. One guy found a finger buried in his garden. Three fingers were brought in during my time there. It seems this is not unusual, although by the time I catalogued the third I thought the universe was sending me a rude gesture. We had a drowned boy of ten who turned out to be alive, which was shocking, but good for the boy, right? We had a scandal where we ran out of space and had to lay bodies outside on the fucking floor while we tried to catch up with the post-mortems. Some enterprising gal or guy took photos of the cadavers and sold them to a daily and it became a scandal. I promise I was already leaving by then, but having your unit in a news cycle for something like that... well, let's just say it wasn't hard.

Did I mention the first time I worked myself out of a job? Hilarious, I—

'Sir, are you paying attention?' The cop snapped his fingers in front of my eyes.

'Get your hands out of my face. I am an artist. How dare you contaminate my process? I am going about my business, the business of art, something which you, with your shock-troop mentality, cannot comprehend. I am making myself into something new, a living sculpture, a breathing installation, work after a master of the form. I am living slime, living excrescence from the moist junction of living beings. I am life itself, or the residue of life that is left after my passing. That is what I'm trying to do, to accomplish, don't you see? I don't know why I'm talking to you. This is not the kind of digestible creation you ingest, is it? You like potboiler paperbacks, coffee adverts and car commercials, don't you? Reality-style shows? When were you last in a museum or gallery? When did you last read a book that wasn't fiction? Do you see why it is futile to stop me, to interrogate me? I am floating above all this. I *made* all this, but not in my own image. If I click my heels, I'll be home. You'll be left trying to explain to your supervisor what you did with the guy on the tube with the blood and the meat. I have done it, copper. I have achieved what I wanted to and you cannot hold me for I have done nothing wrong.'

I finally took a breath. Whatever happened to shutting up?

The door swung open and a guy brandished a sheet of paper. 'It's not human. It's pork.'

'It looks like you're free to go, sir,' said the cop. 'In future, wrap your meat better.'

'Can I have it back?'

'I'm afraid we incinerated it, sir.'

I nodded.

I clicked my heels, and I was at home, lickety-split.

18

Unlike my normal practice of writing in longhand, I sat at a keyboard and typed, words just pouring out of me. Drops of blood kept appearing between the keys, and there was a hiss between my ears, but I didn't stop writing. I heard the doorbell a few times, but ignored it. I did not eat or drink.

The smell of rot suffused the house because of the pork chops I left in the kitchen outside the freezer. The fleshy statue was pig. I added a bit about Pigmeat Markham, probably the first 'rapper' in hip-hop history. Hip hop is important to my personal history. You know how people in secondary school have 'things' that make them stand out? Well mine was hip hop and breakdancing. Maybe five other people had this interest at the time, that is, in performing, not consuming. I was young, and songs were long. It wasn't unusual for a rap song to have five verses, and there was no Google. We had to start and stop the song to get the lyrics.

I had a good memory and wicked delivery. I had original songs. I was in a band with five other people called the Krazy Krew, which worked well until our lead singer and drummer both got done for drunkenness.

Illegal parties were a big thing when we were in school. We were constantly looking for ways to breach lights-out and indulge in youthful shenanigans. We would dance, we would smoke (cigarettes, not weed), and we would drink alcohol. In fact, I got suspended once in what we dubbed the Johnnie Walker Incident, but that's for another memoir.

On this occasion, one of us, I don't remember who, had the brilliant idea of throwing a party in the centre of the football field. It was unlit at night and nobody would suspect because nobody looked in that direction. One feature of these parties was to keep the music ultra-low volume; not like the silent discos that the young folk have these days with headphones and streaming playlists, but a forerunner.

Anyway. Night in question, I got malaria. Bad. Nothing I could do to rouse myself. My girlfriend even snuck into the boys' hostel to see me, but it was of no consequence. I was out for the proverbial count. I could *hear* the party from the open window in my room, carried on the wind, but I fell asleep. Turns out they got drunk.

I don't know. I'm just glad I was ill, because if not for *plasmodium falciparum*, I'd have been there for the music. I didn't drink back then, so I wouldn't have got drunk, but because my girlfriend came to the hostel after lights out, there were rumours that I was at the party and just didn't get caught.

With my other Krazy Krew members in the equivalent of social jail, I became a solo act, which I parleyed into what passes for popularity in secondary school. I was learning about people and what they respect.

My mother visited me at school, found out I was consorting with drunkards and was… displeased. But then someone, one of the teachers, told her I was a genius. I wasn't. I just knew how to take standardised examinations, which, no matter what anyone tells you, is a separate skill, distinct from intelligence.

When my mum realised she had a genius demon-child, her attitude changed. All of a sudden I had value to her. Bragging rights.

The lesson I learned was that I had to earn love which, fuck that. And fuck boarding school.

The words kept pouring from my keyboard into the novella. They were still meaningless, but this time I was sure they were *new* and meaningless, unlike before. Every thousand words, I would pause and email to Wisconsin. Nothing would stop me.

There's a song by Tom Tom Club called 'Wordy Rappinghood' that seemed to capture what I was thinking and going through. I wasn't thinking anything and words were going through me. The words didn't mean what I thought they meant, and I couldn't bend them to my will anymore.

Whatever the fuck I was writing, I was almost there when I heard the door downstairs open. I looked around me. The nest was there, but the sculpture, the pig, was in pieces in the kitchen.

Footfalls. People were coming in.

'God! What's that stench?' someone said.

'That's what it's been like.' Elise. 'Although this smells more ripe.'

I stole one more look at the screen. So close to the end. So close. I rushed down the stairs.

'What are you doing here? I don't like people in my space when I'm creating. It contaminates my inspiration.'

They stared at me like I was Pennywise, like they were ready to bolt if I made any move to obstruct their exit.

Elise. At least, I thought it was Elise. This was brunette with blue-grey eyes and a wedding ring. She seemed familiar, so, let's call her Elise.

With her, a woman I recognised as a social worker. And two strangers, but I could tell they were doctors. We can smell our own kind.

'I know what this is,' I said. 'But you're mistaken, so leave.'

'Why don't we sit down,' said the social worker.

'Where?' asked Elise.

She had a point. The furniture was out in the yard, water-soaked. I had expanded the original cage and built a throne on a dais in the middle of it. I had sewn together some cloth and dyed it in an acrylic mixture approximating purple. I sat in there and screamed for hours on end when my fingers ached too much from typing. I always left with ideas crawling out of my ears. They were like wisps of smoke because I couldn't capture them in words when I sat down to write.

I... that's what I did in lieu of rest. I wrote, screamed, wrote, screamed, wrote. I hadn't slept in days and the rotting pork wasn't the only source of rottenness.

'This is a Mental Health Act assessment,' said the social worker.

'I know. Didn't I just say I knew what this was?' I said.

'Your wife has concerns.'

'My wife doesn't live here anymore,' I said. 'If she's really my wife.' Shouldn't have said that.

Didn't I say shut the fuck up, Thompson?

Yeah, there wasn't a lot I could do.

Elises's account, the house, my physical state, my refusal to accept help, it was all enough for them to detain me under section two of the Mental Health Act. Unsurprisingly, the police were outside to facilitate a smooth transition from home to a mental health unit. Because of who I was, they did not take me to the nearest facility, which was where I worked.

The first thing that happens to you when you get detained, or sectioned as the common parlance has it, is you speak to a nurse who may read you your rights, called Section 132, and so on. Then you get a doctor, usually a junior one, who clerks you, by which I mean he asks you a whole bunch of questions, examines you, and pokes you with a needle to get blood and stuff. You don't have to answer any of the questions, but then you run the risk of someone using an educated guess to diagnose and treat you, which means you want to gamble your life on twenty-first-century medical wisdom in the United Kingdom. Good luck.

They had given me some hospital pyjamas to wear because my clothes were falling apart when they got me. I still stank, but I looked better. I needed a shower and a shave. I just wanted to finish my book.

'I just want to finish my book,' I said to the young man.

'Of course. And we want you to be able to finish your book. Any medical conditions?'

'Asthma, hay fever, non-specific skin allergies.'

While he wrote, he said, 'Would I have read anything you've written?'

'With the Royal College membership exams coming up? I'm pretty sure you haven't.'

He examined me.

'Squeeze my hand,' he said, checking the power of my grip; standard neurological examination. Then he showed mild concern. 'Hmm.'

'What?'

'There's a huge difference between the power on the right and left.'

Clickety-click, lickety-split, I was in a clicking CT scan machine for his next trick.

'Dr Thompson,' said the radiographer.

'Yes.'

'You are going to need surgery.'

19

It's amazing how quickly people forgive you when they think you're going to die or be changed fundamentally, not for the better, by a surgical procedure. It wasn't brain surgery, not exactly, but it was going to be performed by a neurosurgeon. Ah, fuck it. It was brain surgery.

Basically, I had a haematoma, a mass made of blood, and it had compressed the front of my brain, specifically the left frontal lobe. It was about the size of a California orange. They thought it had been there for months. Remember when I fell down the step ladder from the attic? Hit my head? You can get this problem from seemingly trivial trauma. I must have had a slow bleed and this orange was the result.

Your humanity is in your frontal lobe. You know when people make speeches and say shit about what separates us from animals, etc., blah blah? Well, I always whisper 'frontal lobe' when I hear or read that.

We know this because of a dude called Phineas Gage, railroad worker, and practically immortal in psychiatry and neurology. I knew his story intimately. Gage was a foreman working on clearing rocky outcroppings from the path of a rail track in Vermont, USA. He determined the placement of explosives. The process was you drilled a hole, you gently packed it with explosives, you covered this with sand, then you tamped it down with a three-foot tamping iron. Gage would have done this many times. On 13 September 1848 he tamped down without the sand for some reason. The rod generated a spark that ignited the dynamite, which turned the rod into a missile that went into Gage's face at the left cheekbone and exited from the crown of his head.

Not only did he survive, he was conscious when taken to a doctor and said, 'Doctor, here is business enough for you.'

His life afterwards is subject to some speculation that hasn't come from primary sources, but it is certain that he was not the same man. Words used to describe him included fitful, profane, irreverent, impatient, obstinate, capricious, where he was not these things before. He died in 1860 or 1861 after developing seizures. You can bet I was worried about the fate that awaited me, but neurosurgery has moved on considerably since the 1860s.

Doctor, here is business enough for you.

A woman called Norton operated on me. She and her team drilled a small hole in my skull and drained the haematoma, relieving the pressure, decompression they call it, and repaired the blood vessels. She played Beethoven, Symphony No.7 in A major, looping through the movements over and over. Oh, yeah, I was awake for this. I didn't want to be, but them's the breaks.

Ms Norton wasn't the chatty kind of surgeon but she had a social media profile that included photographs of weddings. Not hers, not people she knew, but an accumulation of random wedding photos from the internet. I didn't see any ring on her finger, but that didn't mean anything. I would probably never know the reason for this obsession.

'Dr Thompson, your symptoms might not go away after the surgery, or they might fade over the next few weeks. The haematoma might come back and you might need another burr hole.

Be vigilant.'

Elise and Trap came to visit me in hospital. Trap was happy to see me and wanted to inspect my wound. Elise was reserved, but understanding.

'GUM clinic for an STI screen next,' she said. 'As soon as you can walk.'

'Yes, I suppose I should.'

At least she was considering the possibility that she might have sex with me again in this lifetime.

Neurosurgery is weird. I was out of there in less than a week. You'd think poking around the old belfry would mean weeks of recuperation, but no. I was prodded by medical students and neuro trainees. I didn't mind. They need to learn.

Destroyer came to see me in hospital the day before I was discharged.

She had timed it so my family had left. I had a conditioned reflex to slouch when I saw her and an intense urge to present my rump. But my forebrain was working again and I knew it was verboten. So did she.

The nurses and support workers glared, and it was obvious they thought this was my trashy side piece.

'I'm sorry, Tade. My work is for consenting adults and I don't think you had the ability to consent.'

'But you're keeping the money, though, right?' I asked.

Her face crumpled.

'That was unfair. You've been very decent to me,' I said. 'I'm just ashamed of myself, of what I've done.'

'You were not yourself,' she said.

In spite of everything, I still felt a stirring. I supposed it would take a while for all symptoms to go. Or perhaps this was just a man responding to a sexy woman type deal. I realised it was going to take me a while to separate out illness from plain lechery.

'But the desires must have been there. The haematoma just removed my self-control. I must have wanted those things.'

'We all want things that self-control says we can't have,' said Destroyer. 'We aren't what we think; we're what we do. And even if you had thought these things in some fleeting way before, you didn't act on them. Don't be hard on yourself, but look me up if you feel like a little self-exploration.'

She brought me posh biscuits and left a miasma of perfume behind. I knew I'd never see her again.

I suppose the first feelings that returned, and I mean emotion now, were variants of mortification. Unlike in the films, I remembered pretty much everything I did while I was... haematomaed, but not in the right order and the details were off, inconsistent, ephemeral.

By my calculations I owed six thousand quid. That just popped back into my head. What happened was I took up gambling. It wasn't hard. The poker app I installed early on in my Francis Bacon journey worked its magic. I won a bit and lost a bit, but never stopped. The phone made it easy and I found the app visually pleasing. The people I played with seemed okay, if they were indeed people and not bots. I played that for two days, didn't think I was getting that Bacon vibe, so the next time I got a beating and a fucking I asked if there was any place for underground gambling nearby.

Long story short, I lost thousands at roulette and baccarat. And dice. I played a little of that too. Unfortunately I didn't have Francis Bacon's deep pockets or a gallery that was willing to float me cash whenever I was short.

I went to my crack house to pay back what I owed there. I had it in cash in a brown envelope. I took it to my guy who looked in and laughed.

'The fuck is this? You owe *twenty* thousand pounds, bruv,' he said.

Ordinarily, this would not have been a problem for me, but when I checked my account... well. It wasn't exactly clean. My consultant's salary was still going in, but the last payment from my employer was all I had left. I checked the breakdowns and there was all sorts of stuff that was going to take me months to disentangle in there.

*

The world after surgery looked like things do just after a rainstorm. Clean, fresh and forgiving. Still fluffy around the edges, and I didn't trust my senses as much as before.

I knew Elise was Elise now, and that Trap was Trap.

Even now, when I try to recall those febrile days before my diagnosis, it's unclear. Locations are indistinct and bleed into each other, people are misidentified, dates are optional extras in what I can only describe as a prolonged psychedelic interlude. I've never tried to retrace my steps because I'm the one who walked them and I have no way of recalling where the haematoma took me. I'm pretty sure I have left some things out of this account.

I was back now.

I knew what the world was.

It was a trick of the light, a thing covered with a veil that is so easily removed by trivial injury to this fragile flesh. With a tap to my head all my decency, my training, my honour, everything that I thought I was peeled away and the animal within emerged. Who then is the true me? The civilised doctor, father, husband, writer? Or what lies beneath?

20

Trap and I went back to our Jot and Tittle superhero work. We drew their adventures on watercolour paper in the exact spot where I had my throne before. It felt good to finish the father-son thing we had started. I felt less shitty and Trap seemed ecstatic.

'Do you know anything about picture books?' Elise asked.

'No, we're just faking it.'

'Till you make it?'

'No, just faking. Faking all the way, no making.'

Elise redecorated everything and sealed off the attic for now. The house smelled of fresh-cut flowers and love.

When I got the phone call, I was sceptical.

'Hi, Tade, it's Marge.'

I couldn't answer at first. Marge was an old girlfriend whom I hadn't talked to for like ten years.

'Tade?'

'Yes?'

'Do you remember who I am?'

'This isn't a good time, Marge.'

'I'll be quick, then. I'm having a ceremony to say farewell to the little spirit. The vicar said it would be prudent to ask if you wanted to be part of it. It's okay if you don't.'

Little spirit. Marge had been twenty-nine weeks pregnant with what would have been our child. She suddenly went into labour and the child could not be saved. The baby lived for forty-three minutes. I remembered it like it only just happened. I was on the verge of tears, but emotional incontinence can be the effect of frontal lobe problems.

'Say something,' I said. I put the phone to Trap's ear.

'Did you hear anything?' I asked.

'A woman,' said Trap.

'Jot and Tittle will have to wait a bit.' I put the phone back to my ear and said, 'I'm listening.'

Elise was surprisingly accommodating and encouraged me to go.

The miscarriage broke us up, Marge and I. She told me she had sunk into bouts of depression and a mild eating disorder. It had taken a long time, but she had climbed out of that snake pit, although she kept falling back in. She said the lost baby was at the centre of it.

'I named her, you know? I call her Renee.' Her voice was heavy, like she had either been crying or was about to start.

'Renee.'

'You don't like it?'

'I love it. I used to call her Daisy in my head.'

Renee Thompson. Forty-three minutes old, but still affecting my life.

Small, weekday ceremony. Marge's mother was there. I got along with her and we hugged for a long time. I hadn't realised how much I missed her.

A decade after the fact, we said goodbye to Renee Daisy Thompson. She has a plaque somewhere in South London and I cried over it. I don't know if it was residual frontal lobe dysfunction or my grief at the death of my first child.

As I said goodbye to Marge for the last time, some kind of weight lifted from her shoulders and mine.

I visit the plaque every year, but not on her birthday. I do it on the anniversary of my brain surgery. I talk to her sometimes. I tell her I'm sorry she couldn't stay, that the world is not great, but that there are great people here. I tell her about her mother's hairy upper lip that she tucks in or hides behind a book because she's ashamed of it. I tell her it suited Marge and that the skin got bumpy when she shaved it. I tell her about Trap and Elise, that she would have loved them. I tell her I've been sick, but that I'm better now, and that I can see life for what it is.

I knew my recovery had progressed well when I browsed a second-hand bookshop on Fulham Road. I found a paperback, *Henrietta*, by Henrietta Moraes. The cover was a Lucian Freud painting. I had no sexual response whatsoever when I saw it, flipped through it, bought it, and read it all through that night. Eventful life. I wondered what she would have made of my experiences.

There's an app you can get that works synergistically with the online poker app. Basically, it patterns your betting and punts for you. I had apparently installed it and gave it no credit limit. That's why I had no money left. I had no recollection of doing this, but I must have.

I took out my SIM card and killed my phone. To this day I no longer use smartphones.

'Double-Tee!' said Tarquin. 'How're we doing with the novella?'

'We're not.'

'What do you mean?'

'I'm not doing the book. It's cursed, Tarquin.'

'Dude.'

'What?'

'It's a great opportunity to—'

'You write it, then. Or get someone else. You have quite a few writers on your slate.'

'You're the one they asked for.'

'Tell them thanks, but no thanks.'

'Tade, don't—'

'Goodbye, Tarquin.'

He got over it.

Especially when *Jot and Tittle* became a surprise illustrated book hit and Trap Thompson's first literary credit. I never took it seriously, but Tarquin came up to the house to beg and while grovelling he came across the concept art.

'What the fuck is this?' he asked.

I saw his eyes dilate and I knew where this was going.

What I didn't realise was how big children's books could be. I'm drawing the third book now and Trap's drafting the words.

Trap and I have made a tidy sum from the books, more than any of my other efforts until now. I'm not rich, but I've paid off my gambling debts with lots left over.

Trap's saving up for college, which is good for me because I would have had to explain to him why I spent all my money on sex workers and gambling.

Of course, he's going to read this someday, so... hmm.

Seen in a bookshop window in Oxford Street: *Jackdaw: Being the memoir of a most interesting assignment by [redacted]*.

I didn't know what to think or feel, so I walked on by.

The whole episode struck me as messy, like 7 Reece Mews. Nanny Lightfoot, sentinel, watching with quiet menace, doing what she did in life, looking out for Francis Bacon, making sure I didn't fuck up the commission, which I did. Me lusting after Henrietta, her disappearing when Destroyer appeared because fantasy dies when reality arrives. Whoever I distorted Elise into and her psychic pain. I don't even know if I really met Bacon's people. At least Tarquin's real; oleaginous, but real.

My story's almost told. I did finally see Francis Bacon, after a fashion.

When I had healed and my physio was done and I no longer needed neurology follow-up clinic, I went back to Dotun, the Ifá priest in Brixton.

'You look different,' he said.

I shrugged. 'Call up my father. I want to speak to him.'

'He isn't there,' said Dotun.

'What? Check again.'

He did. Same result.

'There's someone else there, though.'

'Who?'

'He won't say.'

'What the hell does he want? Tell him to get the fuck out of the way.'

'He says "you did well" and "good bye". No, not that. He says "cheerio".'

I went hot and cold at once, then I got up and left. On the train home I closed my eyes for long periods just to reassure myself that Henrietta Moraes wasn't back.

From time to time, I'd get panic attacks, thinking Jessie Lightfoot was in the corner, but she wasn't.

There was nothing left of Francis Bacon in my house except the *New York Times* review of my book that mentioned Screaming Popes.

I threw it out.

And I knew peace.

Acknowledgements

Though I've been writing books for a while, *Jackdaw* is unlike anything I've ever attempted, and I refuse to take the fall alone. I may not have an alibi, but I do have accomplices.

Tarquin Wimmins-Tuffet got me into this mess in the first place. Stay oleaginous, brother.

Thanks to Alexander Cochran, Harriet Vyner, Clare Conville, Darren Biabowe Barnes, Rachel Goldblatt, Anna Weguelin and the entire CHEERIO and C&W team.

Thanks to my family in advance for putting up with whatever discomfort this book generates. Try to remember that this is a novel, and that I flayed my fictional namesake more than any of you.